Charlie's Raven

written and illustrated by

Jean Craighead George

SCHOLASTIC INC.

New York Toronto London Auckland Sydney
Mexico City New Delhi Hong Kong Buenos Aires

Charlie's Raven

Contents

Charlie's Raven

CHAPTER ONE

Blue Sky

Charlie pulled himself one limb closer to the ravens' nest in the lodgepole pine tree.

He had to get a baby raven. Singing Bird, his Teton Sioux Indian friend, had told him ravens could cure people. Granddad was ill. Granddad must have a raven.

About an hour ago, he had seen the raven pair that nested on Bison Butte fly off toward the river. Later when he was closing the gate to keep the bison out of Granddad's ranch, he saw the pair return. They came back to the exact same spot in the exact same tree.

"Babies," he said out loud. "They're feeding baby ravens. Great!" Wiping the sweat from his suntanned cheeks, he noted that the nest tree was the tallest, densest one on the butte. He ran to the pump house and picked up a cardboard boot box, then jogged down Granddad's dirt road to Sagebrush Flats Road. From there he walked to Cache Creek. Hopping from stone to boulder, he crossed the lively stream and worked his way up steep Bison Butte to the meadow and the regal lodgepole pine. He climbed to the nest.

If he could bring a raven home to Granddad, he would get well. He had a heart attack last winter and was not get-

ting better. Singing Bird, his Teton Sioux classmate and neighbor, had told him ravens could cure. Like Charlie, Singing Bird was thirteen. She was studying to be a Teton Sioux storyteller, and part of her training was to tell Sioux tales when the wisdom of a story was needed.

That ravens could cure was wisdom Charlie needed. He loved his granddad very much. Charlie leaned toward the nest. Two nestlings stretched up their heads and opened their beaks to be fed.

"Soon," he said and smiled.

Suddenly a wind hit Charlie so hard he had to wrap his arms around a branch of the tree to keep from falling. The limber tree trunk bent with the blast, and he rode down with it. The valley appeared to tilt up on end. The wind stopped, and the tree and Charlie whipped back in place. The valley was normal again. Feeling dizzy, Charlie looked for the Grand Teton Mountains to stabilize himself. They were not there. A yellow fog obscured them. Eerie.

Gee, maybe the people who think ravens are supernatural are right, he mused. Yellow fog and a rogue wind while I'm robbing a raven nest. The strange wind gusted again and the tree bent low. As Charlie rode back with it he gasped. On a limb above the nest sat the parent ravens. He had not seen or heard them return. But there they were—seemingly metamorphosed from the pine needles. They held their heads high like royalty. Their black eyes looked right at him. He shivered.

Charlie picked up a nestling. The parents lifted the long feathers on the top of their heads until they looked like devil horns. Their throat feathers puffed out like lion manes, and their large beaks were slightly open. Charlie could see the insides of their mouths. They were black. He had never seen black inside a bird's mouth. Most were pink or red. A chill ran down his spine. And something else was eerie. The parents did not scream and dive at him. Bird parents never let an enemy come so near their nest without putting up a fight. Even the tiny hummingbirds in Granddad's yard dive-bombed him when he walked near their nest, and the mother red-tailed hawk had strafed him just for sitting on a rock near her nest tree. In fact, he had worn his winter parka today because he expected an attack from the powerful ravens. Now, it seemed he didn't need it.

A pinecone hit Charlie on the head. Another stung his face. A third got him in the ear. He looked up. The wind had stopped. It was not knocking off the cones, and the red squirrels were not dropping them. He glanced at the ravens.

They were sitting quietly. Then the female, the one who held her head lower than the other, snapped off a cone with her beak, reared her head back, and with a flick of her neck hurled it at Charlie. It struck him on the forehead.

"Wow," he said aloud. "You guys use weapons! No fair!" He pulled the parka hood over his head and picked up a baby raven. It was a funny little thing with big eyes and bits of white down sticking out of its newly feathered head. The little bird seemed perfectly content in Charlie's hand. Another pinecone hit Charlie. Then everything changed. The parents screamed the raven alarm cry—"KEK,KEK,KEK, KEK,KEK,KEK."

The baby raven croaked and flapped his stubby wings. Charlie hurriedly tucked him inside his parka so he couldn't see. Like all daytime birds in the dark, he would sit still and be quiet. As Charlie backed down the tree, pinecones pelted him and raven alarms rang out.

When he was halfway to the ground, the parents stopped the pinecone war. Their alarms ceased. What did that mean? Charlie asked himself. Were they going to dive-bomb him now? He pulled his parka hood over his head, then backed on down the tree and dropped to the forest floor.

Charlie scanned the butte. No ravens were to be seen or heard. He carefully removed the youngster from his parka and placed him in the boot box lined with an old towel. He closed the lid. Not a sound came from the little bird. Not a sound came from his parents.

Charlie wondered if the silence meant that the ravens

were plotting some terrible revenge. He was about to return the baby bird when he recalled Singing Bird's story.

"One day, long ago, just before the flowers of the buffalo grass bloomed, a young Teton Sioux woman fell ill. Although the medicine man fed her herbs, she did not get better. One morning her husband asked White Buffalo Calf Woman, the spiritual leader of his nation, to save her.

" 'Bring a raven into your teepee,' she said. 'Ravens cure.'

" 'Ravens live in the forests,' the husband replied. 'We live on the prairie. Where will I find a raven?'

" 'Ride west,' the White Buffalo Calf Woman said and departed.

"That very morning the husband mounted his horse and rode across the grassy plains. He rode day and night until he came to a butte where trees grew and ravens lived. He climbed to a nest in a tall tree and took a baby raven, then swiftly climbed down. The parent ravens yelled "KEK, KEK,KEK,KEK,KEK" and dive-bombed him until he was far away. Galloping hard, the husband reached his teepee at dawn and placed the little raven by his wife.

"When the buffalo grass was in full bloom, the young woman was well."

Charlie believed Singing Bird and her story. The Teton Sioux had lived on the prairie for a good ten thousand years and knew more about the animals and plants than all the field guide books in the library. If they said a raven could cure, then it could. Besides, there was something special about ravens, something intelligent and mysterious. He hugged the box close to his chest and jogged down the butte to Cache Creek, crossed it, and, looking back over his shoulder for the ravens, trotted to the county road.

"Ravens are good," he heard Singing Bird say. But he also remembered that Granddad's new neighbor, Mr. Spinder, had the exact opposite opinion. He and his wife lived about a mile down the road from Granddad in the log house by Cache Creek. Only sagebrush and bison lay between the two homes in the valley walled by the granite mountains of the Tetons on the west and Shadow Mountain on the east.

Mr. Spinder and his wife were a new kind of resident on Sagebrush Flats. They never used first names, theirs or anyone else's. They wore fancy chaps with fringed shirts and expensive Stetson hats when they rode their magnificent Appaloosa horses. They drove a big SUV. Their obvious wealth put a distance between them and the other residents and barred familiarity.

Charlie had learned a little bit about the couple when he met Mrs. Spinder in the post office. She told him she and her husband liked their new home in "this quiet valley" and that they were from a large city. Charlie understood why city dwellers might find Sagebrush Flats quiet, although he and his granddad found it excitingly noisy. Their glorious valley resounded with the caterwauls of mountain lions, the piercing cries of eagles, the bugling of elk, and the trilling songs of birds.

After that he gave the Spinders little more thought until he found Mr. Spinder waiting for him one morning at the gates of the irrigation ditch where the local landowners met almost daily to release water to their land. Mr. Spinder got off his horse when he saw Charlie arriving through the green-gray sagebrush. Mourning cloak butterflies burst up around him. A pronghorn antelope that had followed the retreating snow up from the lowlands into the high valley at the foot of the Tetons skittered away as Charlie came near.

"Hi," Charlie said to Mr. Spinder. "I'm Charlie Carlisle. My granddad is your nearest neighbor."

"Howdy," said Mr. Spinder.

"We're about a mile down the road from you." Just then something strange happened. A raven circled overhead and dropped onto a dead limb of a nearby cottonwood tree. The man saw it and walked closer to Charlie. He was nervous, almost frightened.

"That bird," he said, pointing, his voice hoarse and low. "It's a raven. Ravens are supernatural. Evil." He turned away from the glossy black bird and leaned toward Charlie. "That bird is bad news."

"He is?" said Charlie.

"I've got a nest behind my house."

"But they're good birds. Really good. You're lucky."

"They are evil," Mr. Spinder repeated, pinning his eyes on Charlie's eyes. "In the beginning these black ravens were beautiful white birds. Then they did wicked things and the gods made them black. They assigned them to the dying."

"I don't know about that," Charlie said, "but my granddad says ravens play an important role in nature. They're good."

"Evil," he repeated. The raven on the cottonwood stretched its ebony wings, and purple and blue lights flashed. The bird stepped out of the sunlight and turned black. Mr. Spinder shuddered and fanned his jowls with a new Stetson hat.

"See that? He's evil," he said. "Changed colors." He reached for his horse. Like the owls whose eyes can't move in their sockets, he turned his whole head to see if Charlie had understood what evil he was seeing. Charlie was smiling.

"It's just the sunlight on his iridescent feathers," he said. "Granddad's a naturalist. He studies them . . . at least he did before he got sick." The raven took off and flew toward them.

Mr. Spinder's eyes widened. He wiped his sweaty hands on his Levi's, mounted his horse, and galloped away. He and the raven headed for Bison Butte. Charlie shrugged, pushed back a swatch of sun-bleached hair from his forehead, and opened the gate in the irrigation ditch. He watched the water sparkle down the dry ditch, headed for Granddad's trees.

Three of the four families on Sagebrush Flats were good friends and helped one another whenever help was needed. Charlie wondered if their new neighbor, who was now a speck in the sagebrush, would also be a friend. If so, he had to learn that ravens were good.

And yet, Charlie mused as he carried the little bird down the dirt road toward Granddad's ranch house, what about that rogue wind that nearly knocked me out of the tree, the pinecone bullets, and the yellow fog that obscured the mountains. Pretty eerie. Nothing like that has ever happened to me before—but then, I've never stolen a baby raven before. . . . Eerie.

As he reached Granddad's private road the yellow fog began fading away. The massive mountains reappeared. They stood resplendent against a vivid blue sky.

"Hey, the sky is blue again!" Charlie exclaimed aloud. "Singing Bird is right." He held the boot box close. "Ravens are good. The fog's gone. The wind's stopped. The pinecone barrage is over—and the sky is bright and blue. Granddad will get well. Little raven, your name is Blue Sky."

He jogged around the green circle of trees that surrounded the ranch house, crossed the bridge over the irrigation ditch, sprinted through the sun-yellow balsamroot flowers, and, breathless, came to a standstill on Granddad's ranch-house porch.

Two adult ravens were perched on the roof, silently staring at him.

CHAPTER TWO

Granddad

Granddad was resting in the stuffed chair that faced the big picture window in the living room of the log home he had built almost sixty years ago. The window faced the majestic Teton Mountains, where the light now played over peaks and forests like sunbirds. Granddad's eyes were closed. A wildflower guidebook lay in his lap. He had written it. Since his heart attack, the famous old naturalist could no longer hike and climb the mountains, but he could walk outside and enjoy the wildflowers on his ranch.

Charlie tiptoed into the living room of the cozy ranch house he had loved as long as he could remember. The walls were hung with Granddad's photos of bear, owls, ravens—all the animals he had studied. Fishing rods stood in corners and pots of native wildflowers bloomed on the window-sills. This summer Charlie was living with Granddad and Grandma until school started. Grandma Sally needed him to do the chores while she took care of Granddad.

Charlie knelt by the big woodstove and took Blue Sky out of his box. The nestling gave a short raspy "gro, gro, gro."

Granddad opened his eyes.

"Hey!" he said. "I heard a baby raven begging for food."

He saw Charlie. "That you, Charlie, sounding like a baby raven?"

"No," he answered. "It is a baby raven. I brought you one. Singing Bird said it would make you well."

Granddad chuckled softly and held out both hands.

"Let me hold him before you take him back. I've studied these birds for many years and still have much to learn. Ravens are the most interesting birds I have ever encountered."

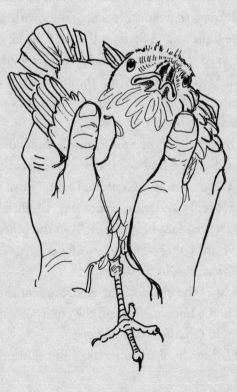

"Why do I have to take him back?" Charlie was upset. "You said you had a permit to keep a raven."

"I do. But I can't do the research anymore."

"But I can," Charlie said eagerly. "I'll put a band on his leg like you do so I can tell him from the other ravens. I'll feed him and take careful notes for you—and I'll. . . ."

"And what will I tell the officials your research project is about?" Granddad asked.

Charlie put Blue Sky in Granddad's hands. The little bird nipped his sleeve. Granddad clucked and stroked the newly feathered head so comically decorated with down. One wisp came loose and floated on the air. Blue Sky cocked his head and eyed it curiously. Charlie's heart went out to the little bird. How could anyone think he was evil. He was solid goodness. With that he knew what he wanted his research project to be.

"Tell the officials," he said to his Granddad, "that I will study Blue Sky and find out if ravens are good or bad."

"Well, there's a dilly," Granddad said. "I can see the National Science Foundation approving of that." But then Granddad's tired face brightened. "On the other hand, you might have an ecology/human study here."

"What's that?" Charlie asked.

"A study of the effect of the environment on humans as opposed to the human effect on the environment."

"Oh," said Charlie. "Well, okay."

Granddad made an effort to stand but slumped back into

his big chair. "Get that unused notebook on my desk and use it for your notes. To begin, write down the date. Also bring the steel ruler from the drawer and we'll measure him. He's about four weeks old by the looks of his feathers.

"It'll be another two weeks before he can fly. He'll eat like mad. You are taking on a big job."

"Two weeks? I hope he stays longer than that," said Charlie. "I need lots of time to find out if he's good or bad." What Charlie was really thinking was that it might take longer than two weeks for Blue Sky to cure Granddad.

Charlie found the notebook and sat down on a low stool beside Granddad.

"You know what?" Charlie said, handing the steel ruler to the old naturalist, "the parents hit me with pinecones. Do I write that down?"

"By all means," exclaimed Granddad, stroking the baby bird. "And write, 'Ravens are tool users.' That's very advanced behavior."

"They fight with weapons," said Charlie. "I think that's bad."

"Don't we?"

"That's different," said Charlie.

"Is it?"

Granddad threw back the quilt that covered his knees and held Blue Sky at eye level.

"gro, gro, GRO, GRO," the little raven yelled.

"Okay, okay," Granddad said to the bright-eyed bird,

and then turned to Charlie. "Write down that his first words were 'I want to eat.' And go to the fridge and get him some food."

"What do I feed him?"

"Mix some fresh eggs with last night's leftover hamburgers. Then break open one of my vitamin pills and add that. And I just heard a mousetrap go off in our bedroom. Go get the mouse. Ravens love them."

June 8, Charlie wrote in the notebook. *Granddad stuffed Blue Sky until he was quiet. Ravens eat mice. That's good. I know how to catch them. A mousetrap set on the little highways they make through the grasses gets them every time.* Then he added, *I think Granddad looks better already.*

Charlie was about to put Blue Sky back in the boot box when the young bird snapped to attention. Without a peep he flattened his feathers to his body. "That's a fear reaction," Granddad said and glanced around the room. He saw nothing that might have scared Blue Sky.

"He's reacting to some stimuli outdoors," Granddad said. "Go look. See if you can find it—and write it down." Charlie opened the door and to his amazement saw Mr. Spinder and his wife riding past Grandad's house on their Appaloosa horses.

"KEK,KEK,KEK,KEK,KEK," cried the two ravens on Granddad's roof. Two more alit near the chimney and kekked. Then all four ravens took off and, flying in close formation like planes at an air show, followed the riders. Charlie ran back to Granddad.

"It was Mr. and Mrs. Spinder," he said. "And four ravens. What does that mean?"

"Write it down."

The door opened, and Grandma Sally came in with two bags of groceries. "Charlie, would you get the sack of oranges and the bottled water from the car, please?" she asked. "And take a look at the six ravens on the roof."

"Six!"

"Write it down," said Granddad enthusiastically as he was drawn into the mysteries of the natural world again. Charlie's eyes widened with pleasure. Granddad was definitely beginning to look and sound better.

"Why six ravens?" he asked the old naturalist.

"Write it down. I don't know what it means. But ravens are social birds, and we are social mammals. Societies form to accomplish things individuals cannot."

"That's pretty weird," said Charlie. "I mean ravens being sort of like us."

When Charlie came back with the oranges and water, the mountains had disappeared behind the strange fog again.

"That's the second cloud of pollen this morning," Granddad said. "The lodgepole pines are telling us something—bad year? good year? or just a lavish effort to survive in view of what we're doing to the environment?"

"Oh," said Charlie to himself. "So that was it. Pollen." The fog he thought the ravens had conjured up was pollen. He laughed and reminded himself to think sensibly from now on. Ravens couldn't brew a yellow fog even if they wanted to.

"QUORK! QUORK! QUORK!" The call came from outside. Granddad straightened up in his chair.

"That's the raven's call in defense of its home territory." Reaching for his cane, he breathed in deeply and stood up. "Why are they defending this property? I've only heard ravens give that call over Bison Butte and other places where they nest."

"Maybe because Blue Sky's here," said Charlie.

"Write that down," said Granddad, proud of his offspring. "I think you're right. But don't conclude that. Just put it down." He teetered unsteadily.

"Be careful, Will," Grandma Sally said. "Sit down." He

did not. "Please, sit down." He walked slowly to his desk for his box of bird banding equipment and carried it to his chair.

"Charlie," he said. "Bring me little Blue Sky."

Charlie put the raven in Granddad's gentle hands. Holding the bird on its back along his arm, Granddad stroked the young raven's breast until Blue Sky was in a trance. Then taking the bird's right leg between his left thumb and fingers, he took a red band from the box and a Fish and Wildlife Service aluminum band with numbers on it. He read the numbers to Charlie, who wrote them in the bird-banding record book. Granddad then pried open each band and slipped them on Blue Sky's leg. He closed them with pliers.

"grrrrrr," said Blue Sky.

"Is he mad?" asked Charlie.

"No. That's his comfort sound. We are doing something right."

"Will," said Grandma Sally. "You must rest." She took his hands in hers. "You're cold." She turned to Charlie.

"Please, take that bird to your cabin. He's exciting Granddad."

"He's going to make him well."

"Make him well? He's making him worse. He's making him do too much."

From the sky above the ranch house came, "KEK,KEK, KEK,KEK,KEK." It was given forcefully and with desperation.

"The raven alarm cry again," Granddad said. "An enemy is near."

A knock sounded on the door. Grandma Sally opened it. There stood Mr. Spinder.

"You have ravens on your roof," he said and stepped inside quickly. As he edged into the seeming security of the kitchen, Granddad whispered to Charlie, "What has Mr. Spinder done to earn the wrath of the ravens?"

"Maybe they know he doesn't like them," said Charlie. "Would they know that? Would that do it?"

"That's part of it. But it must be more—he must have shot or poisoned them."

"Gee, I hope not," Charlie said and put the lid on the box where Blue Sky rested. He did not want the little bird to call out and arouse Mr. Spinder's fears.

"Please, Mr. Spinder," he heard Grandma Sally say. "Come sit down out of my husband's hearing. He's not well. You can tell me what your problem is." Grandma Sally ran her fingers through her short gray curls and took off her glasses. She was a small vibrant woman with the energy of a den of chipmunks. Mr. Spinder took a seat at the dining table, and Grandma Sally opened a box of her homemade cookies. Glancing over the kitchen counter into the living room, she saw that Will was resting in his chair. Charlie was taking notes.

"Now, what's your problem?" she asked. "You look very worried." Mr. Spinder took two cookies.

"I am. There are ravens in our neighborhood. They are an evil menace. They poke holes in roofs. They dive at people's eyes and hair. We must get rid of them." The jowls on his marmot-shaped face shook.

Grandma Sally did not reply. Instead she called to Charlie in family code, "How's Granddad?"

Charlie knew by the evenness of her tone that she was saying, "I want to get rid of Mr. Spinder as gracefully as possible. Make an excuse." Quicker than a toad's tongue snagging a fly, Charlie called, "Granddad needs to sleep, Grandma. Can you help me get him to his bed?"

Mr. Spinder got to his feet. "I'd better go," he said and turned to Grandma Sally. "Put rotenone poison in bread and throw it out for the ravens."

"But that's illegal," she said. "Ravens are federally protected."

He walked to the door, and with the heels of his cowboy boots clicking on the pine floorboards, he exited.

"KEK,KEK,KEK,KEK,KEK,KEK."

Charlie rushed out to see what was happening. Six ravens flew high above the road, "kekking" and warning the neighborhood about Mr. Spinder. They did not stop their harassment until he had ridden his horse all the way through his gate and disappeared inside his house. When the ravens could no longer see him, they broke ranks and flew in pairs back to their respective territories. Charlie ran to Granddad.

"I know Mr. Spinder doesn't like ravens," he said. "But the ravens don't like him either."

Granddad's eyes shone brightly. "Something's going on

here," he said. "Birds are able to recognize individual people. These ravens know Mr. Spinder all right. I'll wager he's been out with his gun. Ravens know all about guns.

"But don't write that down. I can't prove it." He leaned back in his chair and closed his eyes.

Charlie took out his pencil and wrote:

Granddad's smiling in his sleep. He's a lot better. Score one for the raven in the Good column. Then he erased the last sentence and wrote: *It's hard to be a scientist. I already love Blue Sky and want him to be good, not evil.*

CHAPTER THREE

Singing Bird

Charlie carried Blue Sky to a small log cabin that stood a weasel leap from the main house. More than a hundred years ago the cabin had been part of the individual tourist motels in Yellowstone National Park. When the park modernized, the superintendent offered the old-fashioned cabins to whomever would haul them away. Granddad and Charlie's father, Chris, had taken three. One was set behind Granddad's big house as a guest house. The other two had been expanded into a home for Chris and his family on the other side of the irrigation ditch. Chris and Nancy Carlisle, and Charlie's little brother, Andy, had lived there until two years ago. Growing up next door to Granddad had been a happy time for Charlie. He often accompanied him on treks to the wilderness to study plants and wildlife. He had scrambled over rocks to track the little pikas, or mountain rabbits, and had climbed trees with him to help put bands on hawks and owls.

Then Charlie graduated from the local grammar school in Morton just down the road. Morton had no middle or upper schools, and so Chris and Nancy Carlisle rented out their cabin and moved to Jackson. In the thriving town Charlie attended the valley's only middle and upper schools,

and Andy went to the Jackson elementary school. This worked out well for Charlie's dad. He could walk to the office of Outdoor Adventure Trips, Inc., his tourist service, which took people down rivers and into the mountains. The business had been growing rapidly in recent years.

Charlie had been devastated by the move, and Granddad knew it. After his heart attack, he and Grandma Sally fixed up the little Yellowstone guest cabin behind the ranch house and put in a new cot, bedside table, bureau and desk, a chair and oil lamps. "The cabin is yours for the summer and whenever you want to come," Granddad told Charlie when he and his mother came to visit one late-spring day after school.

"Really?" said Charlie. He opened the door and stood there transfixed. "I love it, love it."

Granddad turned to Nancy. "I can use Charlie's help," he said to the pretty woman, who never wore anything but blue jeans and western shirts, even to parties. "Is this arrangement okay with you and Chris?"

"It's wonderful!" she said. "Charlie's not happy in town, especially in summer. Visiting here on weekends isn't long enough for him. He's missed you and the outdoors. Andy is very different," she went on. "He's happiest in groups and playing sports. Little League, swimming, skateboarding, snowboarding, are his dish of huckleberries.

"Maybe Charlie can even help you with your raven study," she said. "The one where you were putting radios on ravens to find where the young went after they left home. I've always wanted to know the answer to that."

"I've given up on that study," Granddad said. "Someone else will have to unlock that mystery."

Charlie moved into the cabin as fast as a chipmunk dives into a woodpile when a hawk is overhead. He spread furs on the floor, hung pictures of falcons and mountain lions on the wall, and put comforters on the cot. Nights were cold in the mountain valley even in summer.

The cabin became Charlie's kingdom. It wasn't large, about twelve feet by twelve feet, and it was dark. The small windows were designed to keep out the grizzly bears of Yellowstone National Park. Its very darkness made the cabin as cozy as a wolf's den.

When he had moved in, Charlie had been worried about Granddad. But now he knew the old naturalist would be all right. He had a raven to cure him. He put the young bird in a bowl-shaped Shawnee Indian basket on the floor and sat down beside him. When the little raven's eyes adjusted to the dim light, he fixed them on Charlie's blue eyes and stared unblinking for almost six minutes. Charlie sensed magic passing between them. He wasn't sure why, but he felt great pleasure. He wrote, *"Looking at me" goes in the Good list.*

"grrrrrr," uttered Blue Sky. The pleasant purrlike sound seemed to come from some deep bird emotion.

"grrrrrr," Charlie said, imitating, then touched the raven's head with his head. "I am saying hello," he said. "This is how the irrigation ditch ravens say hello to each other." He touched heads again.

Blue Sky lifted his feathers and shook in reply. Then he tucked his beak in the feathers on his back and closed his eyes.

Many hours later Charlie wrote in his notebook.

June 8. It's 1:30 p.m. I fed and talked to Blue Sky. Then we looked at each other for a long time, and magic happened between us. I mustn't tell Granddad. Too unscientific—but it did.

For the next week Charlie had a companion while he did his chores. The little raven, who was still too young to fly, walked behind him wherever he went and tried to do everything he did. When Charlie pulled weeds out of the irrigation ditch, Blue Sky took a weed in his beak and pulled too. When Charlie split kindling for Grandma Sally, Blue Sky picked up the wood chips. When Charlie inflated the raft in the boathouse for a ride down the Snake River, Blue Sky sat on the oarlock and flapped his wings. When Charlie primed the pump in the pump house, Blue Sky whacked the pipes with his beak. Charlie removed one screw from a can of screws to fix Grandma Sally's bird feeder, and Blue Sky walked up to the can and tossed the rest around the pump house. Charlie spent an hour finding and putting them back.

Under Bad he wrote in his notebook: *Tosses screws out of can.*

One day Nancy came to the ranch to be with Granddad while Grandma Sally drove to Idaho Falls for supplies. Blue Sky ran across the floor to her and whacked her shoe so hard she cried out.

"Whoa," said Charlie and picked up the bird. "That's bad. That's another one for the Bad column."

"I think he's jealous of me," Nancy said and chuckled. "You pay too much attention to me."

At the end of each day Charlie would take the little raven to his cabin and sit down with him. Blue Sky would cuddle on his lap and contentedly rest his head on Charlie's leg. Then he would emit soft sounds of affection—"kmmmm grrrs." Charlie felt their meaning and would tell Blue Sky he loved him too by picking him up and whispering "kmmmm grrrs" into his sweet-smelling feathers. One night Charlie wrote:

When I hold Blue Sky close, he closes his eyes halfway and bunts me with his head. I think that means he loves me too. Charlie started to erase the last sentence as unscientific, then added, *I say love. That's putting human thoughts in him, but I don't know any other word to use because I am a human.*

Blue Sky and Charlie came to breakfast at Granddad's house every morning. Before sitting down at the table Charlie would place Blue Sky on Granddad's knee for a greeting—bumping heads—and a "chat." One morning Blue Sky stared at Granddad, lifted all his body and back feathers, and uttered, "knock, knock knock."

"That's the power feather display and the power call of the raven," Granddad said. "Very interesting."

June 17. Granddad is special to Blue Sky. He feels differently about me, however. He says "kmmmm and grrr" to me. That's because he is imprinted on me. I am his mother. I think that happened in his head the day he gazed into my eyes. He was kind of photographing my face on his brain, the face that was taking care of him. He says something else to Granddad—the power call. I hope it is what I think it is—"the raven cure."

Every day after that Charlie watched to see if Blue Sky's "knock, knock, knock" was the raven magic that would make Granddad better.

One night he wrote:

Granddad smiles when Blue Sky "knocks," but Grand-dad is not getting well as fast as the Teton Sioux woman did. I wish he would. I want to go with him to the bald eagle nest. They have young now. I want to raft the Snake River and count the osprey and geese with him again and I want to climb the butte with him to find the first locoweed. We had fun.

Blue Sky's wing feathers kept growing. When they were as long as an adult raven's, he changed his routine. In the morning before breakfast, Blue Sky stood up in his basket and scratched the back of his head with a toenail. He then stretched one wing and leg, pulling and releasing the muscles, and then the other wing and leg. Finally he sat on the rim of his basket and flapped both wings so vigorously Charlie thought he would fly. But he didn't.

"All this seems more like growing up than 'good' or 'bad,'" he wrote one morning and added, *"Dad's coming out today. He raised a baby crow and might know what's going on, because crows are in the same family as the ravens, and they act a lot alike."*

A knock sounded at his door.
"It's me, Singing Bird. Let's go fishing."
Charlie opened the door a crack and peered out. There stood his very best friend, Singing Bird. The two of them had met in second grade when her parents bought land and

built a ranch house across the irrigation ditch from Grand-dad. Her parents had seen the Grand Teton Mountains when they were first married and pledged that somehow, some way, they must live near those majestic snowcapped peaks. Although the Teton Sioux Nation had never lived in the valley below these mountains, Singing Bird's parents felt a kinship with them. The Indian name *Teton* came from Tutonwan, one of the Teton Sioux tribes that lived along a river. It meant "people in community."

School separated Singing Bird and Charlie when Charlie's family moved to Jackson and Singing Bird's parents returned to the Standing Rock Reservation in South Dakota for the school year. But each spring Singing Bird and her family came back to Sagebrush Flats when school was out.

"Hey," Charlie said, his eyes almost closed by his big smile. "When did you get back?"

"Yesterday," said Singing Bird. "The balsamroot is blooming. We always come back when it blooms."

Charlie was more than happy to see her. Not only was she a good fisherman and a nifty storyteller, but she was also an observant naturalist. He needed her on his study.

"The caddis flies are hatching," she said. "The cutthroat trout will be biting in Cache Creek. Come on out."

Singing Bird wore her long hair in two braids with beautiful black and brown feathers of the prairie chicken tied near their ends. Her bronze cheeks glowed, and her large eyes were as dark as Gentian Canyon in a storm. Slender eyebrows arched over them, emphasizing her pretty face. Silver squash blossom earrings dangled from her lobes. This morning Singing Bird wore her fishing outfit, a pair of faded and frayed blue jeans and a T-shirt that said: STANDING ROCK MIDDLE SCHOOL GIRLS' AND BOYS' BASEBALL TEAM. Charlie stepped out the door and quickly closed it behind him.

"Where's your fishing rod?" Singing Bird asked. Charlie usually appeared at his door with his rod and creel when she called. Now he looked sneaky, as if he had been caught with his hand in the cookie jar. "What's the matter?" she asked.

"I can't come with you," he said. "I'm doing a scientific study."

Singing Bird smiled. "You are? What's it about?"

"Ravens. I am studying ravens for Granddad."

"Ravens." Her eyes brightened. "Can I help? I love ravens. They're magical."

Charlie frowned. She sounded like Mr. Spinder—magical, supernatural, all that unscientific stuff—then he remembered that it was she who had inspired him to get a raven because it could cure, and he opened the cabin door to her.

Blue Sky was sitting contentedly in his basket. He wagged his tail and backed up toward Singing Bird.

"He likes you," Charlie said. "His tail is wagging."

"That means he wants to give me his little diaper bag so I'll carry it far from the nest. Baby birds do this to keep their nests clean of whitewash so predators won't find them."

Quickly Singing Bird took a tissue from her pocket and

held it under Blue Sky. He deposited the aines. She carried it outside and threw it into a patch of scarlet gilia.

Charlie was impressed.

"Where did you learn that?" he asked.

"Teton Sioux knowledge. We live on earth with the birds and beasts."

"Cool," Charlie said. "He's been wagging his tail like that ever since I got him, but I didn't know what he was saying. I just cleaned up after him. Neat. Now I don't have to.

"Want to help feed him? His name's Blue Sky." He wanted to tell her about his study but thought it was better not to let her in on the Good and Bad business. He was sure she would only see good in the raven.

Blue Sky fluttered his wings and begged for food.

"He wants to eat," Singing Bird said, reading his body language. "My dad caught two mice last night. Let's get them."

Charlie was about to close the door when Blue Sky hopped from his basket and ran, wings up, to join them.

"He is coming with us," Charlie said. "He follows me wherever I go and does everything I do."

"You're his mom." She laughed. "All babies think the one who feeds them is their mom, even if they don't look like them. Let me tell you a story."

"After we feed Blue Sky," he said, and led her out the door.

CHAPTER FOUR

The Teepee

Blue Sky rode on Charlie's shoulder as far as the border of Singing Bird's property, where he fluttered to the ground. After flipping a beetle on its back, the young bird strutted proudly between the two friends right up to the door of the teepee.

Singing Bird's father, Flying Cloud, had erected the teepee not far from his ranch house. The native home was both a museum and an office. Singing Bird's parents were authorities on American Indian dances, teepees, artifacts, and customs. They made their living performing Teton Sioux dances for tourists at the Yellowstone Lodge twenty-five miles north. They were also writing a book on the three Sioux Nations, the Tetons, Lakotas, and Dakotas.

Every detail of the teepee was traditional. Soaring Swallow, Singing Bird's mother, had painted the brown and black bison on the outside. Flying Cloud had made the inside furnishings, beds, willow rod backrests, bows and arrows. The home was a national treasure and a sacred place to the people of the first nations. Flying Cloud and Soaring Swallow's American names were Jim and Elaine Kenton, but they rarely used them, preferring their Teton Sioux names.

Singing Bird paused at the round door in the canvas teepee.

"You can't bring Blue Sky in," she said. "He might mess, and Dad would have a fit. Leave him at the door. He'll stay where you leave him. Little birds obey their moms." Charlie hesitated.

"It's okay," Singing Bird said. "He'll wait."

"Well, if you say so." Charlie put Blue Sky by the teepee door where the bird could see him and not wander away looking for his "mom."

"And Charlie," she said as she pushed back the round canvas door, "remember to move to the left. Men move to the left. Women to the right." She chuckled. "Dad sticks by the old traditions. Kinda fun."

Charlie stepped into the spacious cone-shaped home and instantly felt at peace. There was order and beauty here.

Flying Cloud was seated in the owner's backrest at the rear south of the teepee. Charlie made his way over the fur-covered floor to him. Observing the etiquette learned from other visits to the teepee, he did not walk in front of the altar. The altar was hard to recognize, being only a small space of bare earth at the west end of the teepee. The Indian nations called it a "square of mellowed earth."

He glanced around. The teepee was symbols from top to bottom. The floor was the earth, the walls the sky, and the poles the Indian trails to the spirit world.

Colors blazed from every furnishing. The drums by the altar shone red and blue. The willow backrests were painted with turquoise and white designs. Rich amber buffalo hides covered the floor. Brightly beaded boxes and moccasins sat on the floor beside piles of furry skins that were beds. The home was beautiful.

"Hi, Charlie," Flying Cloud said, patting the floor. "Sit down." He was seated cross-legged, repairing the porcupine quillwork on a pair of antique moccasins. He wore a red western shirt, blue jeans, and cowboy boots. His dark hair was tied back in a ponytail. His face was lean and sharply chiseled.

"What's up?" he asked Singing Bird.

"What did you do with the mice you caught last night?" she asked.

"They're in a brown bag in the trash," he said. "What do you want them for?"

"Charlie's raven," she answered and ran off to get them.

"You have a raven, Charlie? That's very good."

"Why is it 'good'?" asked Charlie in a rush.

"They are very important birds in the Sioux world."

"Why? Do they cure the sick?"

"That's the legend, but they were also friends of warriors. Look here." He opened a hide box and took out a small black drum.

"This drum belonged to the Kangi Yuha Tribe, or Raven Owners. They were a warrior society." Charlie took it in his hands. It was small and smooth and smelled of the smoke of sagebrush. He had always admired native drums, even the cheap reproductions in the tourist shops, but this one was art. An exquisitely decorated skin was stretched across the top. The band around it was painted with ravens in all positions. Charlie turned it over, and as he did, it was so sensitive that it resonated like a wind song. "Wow," he murmured.

"These drums could only be owned by special men," Flying Cloud said. "Raven Owners had to know the mysteries of Raven."

"Did their ravens cure people?" Charlie asked eagerly.

"Until the white man brought us smallpox and measles."

Flying Cloud returned the drum to the box and took out a short lance. It was decorated with otter skin and raven feathers.

"The Sash Wearers of the Raven Owners Tribe carried these," Flying Cloud said, turning it so Charlie could see its details. "When they went to war, they thrust these little

lances through their clothing and pinned themselves down. They were not allowed to retreat in battle unless the lances were removed by a friend." He smiled. "I still don't understand how that worked."

"Did they keep ravens?" Charlie asked.

"Occasionally. When the enemy was coming, the tame ravens warned them with, 'KEK,KEK,KEK,KEK.'"

"Enemy," Charlie said. "Ravens do know enemies, don't they?"

"Oh, yes, human enemies as well as wild ones. They can read intent."

Hmm, thought Charlie. Maybe the Bison Butte ravens gave the alarm cry when they saw Mr. Spinder because they knew he wanted to kill them. That would explain their fury.

Flying Cloud put the lance beside the drum in the box and closed the rawhide lid.

"grrrrrr," Charlie said, imitating Blue Sky, then by way of explanation said, "Raven comfort sounds." He looked toward the door.

"Excuse me," he said. "I don't see my little raven. I'd better check on him."

"I'm coming with you," Flying Cloud said. "I want to meet that fellow." He followed Charlie into the sunlight.

"He's gone!" Charlie cried. Singing Bird joined them, the mice in her pocket.

"He can't be gone," she said. "He can't fly." She looked behind the yellow flowering hawkweed. No Blue Sky.

"Maybe he can fly," Flying Cloud suggested and looked in the trees.

"But he can't," Charlie said. "Granddad says his feathers are too soft to hold him."

"Maybe not," said Singing Bird. "I'll bet he can fly and he's in your granddad's trees." Her slender legs sped her along as rapidly as if she were trying to score a home run. She leaped the irrigation ditch and scrambled to the lowest limb of a big cottonwood. She searched the tree. No Blue Sky.

Charlie followed behind. He, too, suspected that the little raven had taken to his wings. He climbed halfway up one of Granddad's big pines and looked among the dense needles for him. Nothing. He came down and searched his cabin. He had left the door ajar. No Blue Sky. He and Singing Bird looked in the boathouse and toolshed. Not a sign of the bird.

"Oh, Singing Bird," Charlie said, holding his head, "how will Granddad get well now?"

"I can't believe Blue Sky's gone," Singing Bird said. "He must be here. Maybe he's hiding."

After several hours of hunting, Charlie and Singing Bird gave up the search and went into the ranch house—both of them almost in tears—and reported to Granddad that the experiment had come to an end.

"Didn't you say there were two youngsters in that nest?" Granddad asked.

"Two, yes."

"Then I guess you'd better go get the other one. We can still go on with our study."

"Really?" Charlie's eyes brightened.

He put on his parka, stuffed a bag of grilled hamburger in his pocket, and he and Singing Bird ran outside and down the dusty road to Sagebrush Flats Road. As they approached Mr. Spinder's ranch a flock of ravens flew over the butte and circled high above the Spinder horse barn. Then one by one the birds dropped out of sight.

"KEK,KEK,KEK,KEK,KEK," screamed the ravens and disappeared.

"There we go again," Charlie said. "The enemy call."

"You said they give that call when they see Mr. or Mrs.

Spinder?" Singing Bird asked. "Well, I just saw a man saddling a horse by the barn. He must be Mr. Spinder, and if I saw him, the ravens saw him. Their eyes are sharper than a surveillance plane."

"Do you think Mr. Spinder killed Blue Sky?" Charlie asked and sucked in his breath. "Is that why they are kekking?"

"Oh, whoa," said Singing Bird. "I hadn't thought of that."

"Unfortunately," lamented Charlie, "Mr. Spinder thinks that's good."

"Let's keep looking," said Singing Bird, and the two climbed the butte in thoughtful silence. They sat under the nest tree of the Bison Butte ravens to rest before Charlie climbed it. The day was hot, the sun brilliant and relentless.

"gro, gro, GRO."

"Hey, that must be the other baby raven," Charlie said. "It's calling for food. I'd know that sound anywhere."

"But it's coming from the ground," Singing Bird said. "Not from up in the tree."

"It must be able to fly," said Charlie. A pinecone hit him on the head.

"We're getting close to the raven baby," Charlie said and rubbed his temple. "That hurt. I'll bet the ravens taught ancient humans how to throw things. Now that's evil." Charlie got to his feet.

"Throwing things is good," said Singing Bird emphatically. "I throw baseballs!" She stood up and circled the nest tree wider and wider, looking for the fledgling.

Charlie stepped back, heard "gro, gro, gro," at his feet, and turned around.

"Singing Bird!" he called. "Here's the other nestling! It's right here on the ground." Singing Bird came running.

Charlie picked it up and looked at its stubby wings. "It must have fallen from the nest. It can't fly."

"It's not afraid of you," Singing Bird said. "That's eerie."

"No, and I know why!" shouted Charlie. "It's Blue Sky!"

"Blue Sky? That's impossible. Are you sure?"

"Look. He's wearing the red and aluminum bands Granddad put on him. Wow. Blue Sky!"

"How in the world did he get here?" Singing Bird asked. "He can't fly."

"I sure don't know," Charlie said. "But he's here."

"Magic," Singing Bird said.

Charlie thought "supernatural" but didn't say so. He gathered up his feathery friend, tucked him under his shirt, and let Singing Bird lead the way down the butte to Cache Creek. They stopped before crossing.

"gro, gro, gro," uttered Blue Sky.

"Okay, little friend, you can eat here."

Charlie sat down by the racing stream that sparkled clear as spring water over the rocks and pebbles. A dipper bird ran along the bottom, snatching up the larvae of blackflies. Charlie was usually fascinated with these swimming and diving birds of mountain streams and waterfalls, but he barely looked at this one. He was intent on restoring his "mother status" with Blue Sky and fed him the hamburger from his pocket until he couldn't open his mouth or even cry.

A strange music sounded from the butte behind them. "quork, quork, quork, trilllll." Charlie looked up in bafflement.

"quork! quork! quork!" came an answer from the trees along Cache Creek.

"Raven talk," Charlie said, and scratched his head.

"What are they saying?" Singing Bird asked.

"I don't know. But Granddad said the way to find out is to watch and see what happens." Charlie held Blue Sky close with one hand and cupped his ear with the other. Singing Bird leaned forward and listened.

The drumlike calls were heard by distant ravens. Several appeared in the sky from seemingly nowhere. They swooped over the Spinder ranch and dropped down on a small meadow uphill from the house. More joined them from the river bottom and Cache Creek.

"Oh, ho," said Charlie. "That 'quork' and trill call brought a lot of ravens. It must mean 'Let's get together and eat.' "

"Looks like it means 'Let's do something bad,' " said Singing Bird.

"Why do you say that? I thought you said ravens were always good."

"Sometimes they gather to knock holes in roofs," said Singing Bird. "These might be gathering to knock holes in the Spinders' roof. Is that good or bad?"

"Holes in Mr. Spinder's roof would be good," said Charlie. "He wants to shoot ravens."

"The year the ravens knocked holes in Mrs. Prettyman's roof everyone said they were bad—except me. I don't like her. She wanted us to take down what she called our 'silly' teepee."

"Looks like good and bad depend on who you are," said Charlie, "but that's not very scientific." He thought a moment, then added, "But that's what it really comes down to."

When the two walked into Granddad's house with Charlie triumphantly holding Blue Sky, Granddad actually got out of his chair. He took the little raven in his hands, grinned, and refused to guess how he had gotten back to his tree home on the butte.

"Don't speculate," he said when Charlie took a guess. "Observe. Take notes." That evening, however, he and Grandma Sally speculated until bedtime about just how Blue Sky might have found his home without flying. They got nowhere.

The next morning Charlie wrote:

July 11. Granddad doesn't want me to guess how Blue Sky got home. Well, I think it's very human to guess, and since this is a study of the environment affecting the human, I'm going to take a guess.

He made a few doodles.

Then he wrote: *I keep thinking "supernatural"—and that's out, out, out.*

"grrrrrr." A raven comfort call. Charlie jumped up from the desk. He checked Blue Sky. He hadn't called. He was asleep. "grrrrrr," sounded again. Blue Sky suddenly awoke and flapped out of his basket. He hopped and fluttered to the door. Charlie was about to catch him when he thought of Granddad.

"No," he said to Blue Sky. "I'm going to OBSERVE." He picked up his binoculars and opened the door.

The little raven walked out, jumped off the log steps, and crossed the yard. He ran, hopped, and walked over the irrigation ditch bridge and into the middle of the dirt road. Exposed to the open sky, the little bird was prey for eagle, hawk, and coyote. He walked on, waddling from side to side as he hurried down the road, with Charlie following behind from sagebrush clump to sagebrush clump to keep out of sight.

"KEK,KEK,KEK." The raven alarm cry! Blue Sky disappeared under a green gentian plant. A golden eagle circled above the spot where he had been, saw nothing and flew on. When the eagle was a speck above the river, an adult raven swooped over the gentian plant. Blue Sky came out of hiding and walked on. The raven flew above him. It was his mother, leading him home.

"So that's how you did it," Charlie exclaimed out loud. "You walked under your raven mother all the way down the roads and up the butte to home!" His eyes glistened with admiration.

July 11, 10 p.m. I did a terrible thing today, Charlie wrote. *I saw Blue Sky's mother leading her lost son home, but I ran down the road, picked him up, and took him back to my cabin. Granddad has to get well. That makes me a "bad" guy to the ravens and a "good" guy to Granddad. This all gets muddier and muddier.*

Charlie closed his notebook, blew out his kerosene lamp, and crawled into bed. He thought about the Raven Owners' drum and the power over life and death that the Native Americans attributed to this bird.

As he fell off to sleep, he heard soft gurgles, feather rustling, and a new sound—"kmmmm gurgle"—coming from the basket. The tone was obvious.

"I love you too," Charlie whispered. "I believe in you. Granddad will get well."

CHAPTER FIVE

Day Care

Every dawn for the next week Blue Sky would announce the sunrise by "gro, gro-ing" for food. Charlie would slide out of bed, dress, and take the young raven to breakfast on his shoulder. The two would enter Granddad's house for what had become an elaborate morning ritual—Blue Sky and Granddad exchanging greetings.

On one of these sunrises Singing Bird knocked on Charlie's door to go fishing. Knowing that the breakfast visit with Granddad would hold up the expedition, Charlie fed Blue Sky in his cabin, put him on his shoulder, and took him along.

They didn't get very far. Blue Sky sulked, put his head low, and drooped his wings. When they had gotten as far as the nest box of the smallest American falcon—the kestrel—attached to Granddad's telephone pole, Singing Bird became alarmed.

"Do you think he's sick?" she asked.

"I think he's mad," Charlie said. "I didn't let him go through the greeting ritual of bumping heads with Grand-dad."

"Could that be?" Singing Bird asked. "Are you saying ravens are like my dad? They have to do everything according to ritual?"

"Looks like it," Charlie said. "Let's go home and find out. We can fish later."

They turned around and went back to the ranch house. As Charlie stepped inside, Blue Sky jumped from his shoulder to the floor and fluttered to the trash basket. He knocked it over with a wing smack. He scattered the papers across the living room floor, shredded an envelope, and tore up a piece of mail before Charlie could stop him. When he finally caught him in both hands, Blue Sky yelled and squawked all the way to the cabin. Charlie closed the door so Blue Sky couldn't leave and returned to help Singing Bird clean up the mess before Grandma Sally came in from weeding her little "hope" garden. "Hope" that the lettuce would not be killed by a summer frost before they could eat it.

Granddad, who had watched Blue Sky's destructive performance, was grinning and sitting up straight in his chair. His lean face looked younger.

"He's mad at you, Charlie," he said.

"Why? I'm his mother!"

"You changed his routine."

The next morning Blue Sky awoke Charlie with his soft love sounds, and Charlie, acting as if nothing had gone wrong yesterday, took him to breakfast at Granddad's. He was going to restore Blue Sky's routine. If Blue Sky was good, Charlie would know that changing his routine turned him into a bad bird. Then he pondered. "But he let me know about it and that's good." He rubbed his chin in confusion.

Once inside the ranch house Blue Sky jumped to Granddad's knee from Charlie's shoulder.

"Hello, beautiful fellow," Granddad said. Blue Sky lifted his "ear" feathers on his head until he looked like a devil.

"You look very well," Granddad said to him, "and very impressive." The horns went down.

"grrrrr," the raven gurgled, then gazed at Granddad with a dreamy, otherworldly look in his eyes. He bowed several times.

"grrrrr," Granddad answered, and touched Blue Sky's head with his forehead.

Blue Sky stood tall and pointed his bill up. He pushed out his chest and spread his wings and tail.

"Look at him," Granddad said spiritedly. "Blue Sky's saying—admire me—I'm incredible."

"He is!" called Grandma Sally from the kitchen.

Granddad looked right into Blue Sky's eyes.

"Hey, Mr. Wonderful, you're six weeks old. It's time you fly."

"gro, gro, gro," Blue Sky said, changing the subject.

"Okay," Charlie said. "I hear you. Time to eat." He was grinning. He had just run an experiment. He now knew that when Blue Sky got his own way, he was "good." Was that bad? he wondered. Getting his own way might save a raven's life and that would be good. Charlie shook his head and carried him to the table.

Grandma Sally had Blue Sky's breakfast ready—two hard-boiled eggs, a piece of French toast, and a mouse she had caught in the trap in the pantry.

"Gee," Charlie said when he saw all the trouble Grandma Sally had gone to in preparing Blue Sky's plate, "this is crazy. Blue Sky has made slaves of us all."

"And willing slaves," Sally said. "I'm getting to love that bird. Your granddad perks up after these morning visits with him. It's amazing." She served Granddad his breakfast in his big chair by the window.

"You look good this morning, Will," she said and smiled.

Blue Sky stood on his own plate, and Grandma Sally fed him everything but the mouse, which Charlie had cut into nice little pieces. The little raven was still not strong enough to tear up a mouse, nor could he swallow it whole as yet. But he sure could eat. His swallowing noises were so loud they carried all the way to Granddad's ear. The old naturalist slipped a small notebook from his breast pocket and jotted something down.

Blue Sky then picked up a piece of mouse, hopped from

the table to the chair to the floor, and walked into the living room. He fluttered up to Granddad's knee and stood before him with the food in his mouth.

"Write this down, Charlie," Granddad said. "He's courting me with a mouse." Granddad bowed like a loving raven and gave the "kmmmm gurgle" love call. Blue Sky ignored him, cocked an eye at the knee blanket, and hid the piece of mouse in a fold.

"Take it all back," Granddad announced in his professional voice. "He's hiding food in the manner of the raven. He is not courting me. He intends to get it for himself when he's hungry.

" 'knock, knock, knock,' " Granddad clucked. Blue Sky ignored him.

"I thought you said 'knock, knock, knock' means 'I am the power,' " Charlie said.

"I was sure it did," Granddad said thoughtfully, "but I guess it depends on who gives it. When he gives the call he gets his way—like demanding to greet me every morning. But when I give it—pooh—nothing."

"Yeah," said Charlie, puzzling over the brain of the bird, but he saw to it that Blue Sky did not miss his greeting ritual for that reason and another. Something was happening between Granddad and Blue Sky. He hoped it was the Teton Sioux cure.

After the morning ceremonies and breakfast, Charlie had his own routines to perform. He carried Blue Sky to his cabin for a nap, opened the irrigation gate, watered the plants, made repairs that were needed, and then set traps to catch mice for raven food. Dr. Bernd Heinrich, the world raven expert, had noted in his book *The Mind of the Raven* the enormous amount of food baby ravens needed every day. A family of four nestlings required six mice, four hen's eggs, two six-ounce cans of cat food, ten ounces of puppy chow, and a couple of scoops of beans. Mice were not always available, so Charlie had substituted canned tuna fish. Divided by four, that was a lot of food, and he was a busy raven mom.

Returning to his cabin after breakfast one morning with Blue Sky on his shoulder, Charlie mulled over their relationship. Because he, Charlie, fed and nutured him, Blue Sky thought that Charlie was his mother and that he looked like him. That's how it was with imprinting. On the other hand, Charlie now realized the change had gone both ways. Taking care of Blue Sky had morphed him into a mother raven.

"If I were Mr. Spinder," he said to Blue Sky, "I would say ravens are supernatural. I'm not a person anymore. I'm a mother raven. And you're not a raven. You're a person." He grinned and was about to go in his cabin when Blue Sky's feet pressed hard on his shoulder—then lifted off. He flapped his wings. Blue Sky was airborne.

"He's flying! He's flying!" Charlie shouted.

"He's flying! He's flying!" shouted Singing Bird as she pushed through the willows, jumped the irrigation ditch, and ran to witness this moment of achievement.

From inside Granddad's house came Grandma Sally's voice. "Will, he's flying."

"Help me get on my feet and out of here," trumpeted Granddad. "I want to see this."

Blue Sky flapped his wings testily, drifted downward, flapped, then soared up and came to rest on the ranch-house roof as Grandma Sally brought Granddad outside.

He didn't see the flight, but he did see his bird friend run to the top of the roof and flap his wings. Ankle deep in blue lupine flowers, Granddad waited for him to fly.

Ten, then fifteen minutes passed. Blue Sky did not fly. Instead he strutted along the top of the roof, thrust his chest out, tilted his head upward, jumped backward, and posed like a Shakespearean actor. Charlie and Singing Bird clapped and cheered while Granddad looked on. Satisfied with his impression on his audience, Blue Sky turned around and looked up.

"Show off," said Grandma Sally.

"He's not showing off," said Charlie. "He's sizing up his new world. That's what he did the first days in my cabin. He'd look at the bed, walk almost up to it and jump back. Finally, when he had figured out the bed wasn't going to pounce on him, he came right up to it. Once he decided that, he didn't pay any more attention to it. Now he is making up his mind about the sky."

"Very good observation, Charlie," Granddad said. "Ravens are cautious. Anything new must be checked out— beds, sky, rooftops, and especially food. Parents have to show young ravens what is good and bad for them."

"Oh, Charlie," said Singing Bird. "That means you'll have to take Blue Sky hunting and show him what he can eat."

"And how do I do that?"

"Bugs are good raven food," she said. "We'll take him out in the sagebrush and teach him to turn over buffalo chips. There are all kinds of goodies under buffalo chips."

"Don't teach him too much," said Grandma Sally. "I want him to stay with us. He's good for Granddad. How do I tell him to stay?"

"Give him this piece of mouse," said Granddad. "You'll be saying 'stick around here, and you'll get more.' " He laughed, teetering unsteadily, and Grandma Sally took his arm.

"I'll do even better than that," Charlie said and stuffed his pockets with dog chow from the pantry. "I'll open a raven restaurant." He climbed on the roof and laid out the banquet.

Blue Sky gave a raspy call and hopped down the roof to the food. He ate, flapped his wings, and walked back to and along the roof ridge. In the shade of the chimney he sat down.

"Look at that," said Singing Bird. "He's making himself at home. Blue Sky knows food means 'please stay.' "

"From now on," said Granddad with a twinkle in his eyes. "Blue Sky will expect crackers and milk on the roof every morning at ten A.M." He took out his little notebook and turned to Charlie. "You know how he is about routines."

"What did you write?" Singing Bird asked him.

"Date, time, behavior."

"I thought you had written—'We have a Day Care Center,' " said Singing Bird.

"I did," Granddad said and winked. Charlie was climbing the porch post again.

"What are you up to now?" Granddad called.

"I'm getting Blue Sky from the roof," he said. "Singing Bird and I are going fishing. I'm going to put him in my cabin. I don't want him to fly away."

"He's not going to fly away," said Granddad. "He's well fed, and besides, you haven't taught him where to hunt. Just leave your cabin door open. When he's ready, he'll go home. It's not your cabin, you know, it's his."

"Look!" said Singing Bird, pointing at the sky. Two ravens were soaring gracefully above the ranch house. They circled twice, as if sizing up the scene below, then banked, rolled completely over, and shot off for the river bottom lands where the valley ravens went to hunt frogs and snakes, salmon flies, and mice at this time of year.

Granddad was right. When Charlie and Singing Bird came home with a stringer of trout and a road-killed ground squirrel for Blue Sky, the little raven was resting quietly in his cabin.

"Good boy," said Charlie. Blue Sky flapped to his shoulder. "gro, gro, gro."

"Okay," said Charlie. "Let's eat."

As they walked the path to the ranch house, Blue Sky flew from Charlie's shoulder and followed a mouse across the yard. Above Grandma's lettuce garden he dove, missed the mouse, and flew back to Charlie.

"Mice are fine, but don't ever pick that lettuce," Charlie said. "That's Grandma Sally's pride. She's never gotten lettuce to grow higher than two inches before a frost kills it.

She thinks this year is going to be different and she'll get us a salad—so don't get any ideas."

Blue Sky sat upright on the back of his chair at the dining table. He lifted all his head feathers until they stood erect like a Teton Sioux warbonnet. His throat hackles shone like black glass.

When he had everyone's attention, he went into a singsong of slow rasping "quorks."

Eager to see the braggart, Granddad got up from his chair, where Grandma Sally had been serving him since his heart attack, and came to the table for dinner.

"You're a handsome cuss, Blue Sky," he said to the elegant raven, and, as if he understood, Blue Sky lowered and lifted his warbonnet and, for the first time, displayed the long black feathers that were his pantaloons.

"Write that down," said Granddad. "He's telling us he's not just wonderful, but terrific."

"He is," said Grandma Sally, who patted Will's hand. "It's nice to have you at the table."

"Well, I'm no better," he said. "Don't take heart. I feel lousy."

"Your color is better," Sally said.

"I like that raven. That's all it is."

CHAPTER SIX

Babysitters

"Charlie!" Singing Bird was pounding on his door and the sun wasn't even up. Charlie rubbed his eyes and rolled to his stomach.

"Ugh!" he huffed. "I'm asleep. What do you want?"

"Why is Blue Sky outside?"

"He's in here."

"No, he's not. He's on the roof. You left him out all night, poor bird."

"He's here."

Charlie came wide awake, slipped on his clothes, and opened the door. Blue Sky, who had been sleeping on the foot of his bed, stretched a wing and leg, then flew to his shoulder. Charlie stepped outside. Singing Bird blew a breath of relief when she saw him.

"Well, then," she said. "You have another raven." She pointed to Granddad's roof. A raven about the size and awkwardness of Blue Sky was halfway down the roof, eating a chopped-up mouse. Charlie had not put it there. He suspected Grandma Sally and grinned. Was she going to keep Blue Sky around for Granddad even if it meant chopping up mice? Had she too decided that ravens could cure? Did she think they were good?

Blue Sky yelled a short and fast "QUORK! QUORK! QUORK!" The call was loud, fierce. He was saying, "Get the devil out of here." He flew from Charlie's shoulder straight to the bird on the roof to see that it did.

The new raven sidled toward him. Blue Sky threw up his "ears" and puffed out his head and throat feathers to say he was boss bird here. The intruder agreed and pulled in its neck. Strutting his stuff, Blue Sky then turned off his "boss" signals and picked up a pine needle from the roof. He presented it to the stranger.

"Hey, they know each other," said Singing Bird. "That's in the Raven Owners' dance. Ravens give gifts to friends."

"Give gifts to friends?" said Charlie. "That goes in the Good column.

"Granddad, Grandma," Charlie called. "Come out. We have a new raven. Blue Sky just registered it for the Day Care Center. He gave it a pine needle."

Granddad shuffled out, leaning on Grandma Sally's arm. He looked up at the birds on the roof and grinned.

"Those two ravens that were circling the house yesterday must have been checking out the center to see if it was good enough for their youngster."

"You mean checking the menu," joked Singing Bird.

Charlie didn't laugh. He kept watching. The birds lifted their feathers slightly and walked side by side. Granddad noted this too.

"They're acting like siblings," Granddad mused. "Let's find out if they are."

"How?" Charlie asked.

"Catch the new raven and we'll band it and get a DNA test on it."

"It can fly," said Charlie. "How do I catch him?"

"In the northeast corner of the toolshed," Granddad said, "is a live trap for large birds. Go get it. We'll bait it, and put it on the roof."

"Suppose we trap Blue Sky instead?" Charlie asked. "He'll probably be furious with me and punish me again."

"Blue Sky will stay inside with me," Granddad said. "It's greeting and breakfast time, and he doesn't like to miss that."

Charlie headed for the toolshed, and Grandma Sally invited Singing Bird in for sausage and biscuits. Blue Sky, no longer feeling threatened by the newcomer, flew down to Granddad and rode into the house on his shoulder. He kept stretching up his head, as if to get it higher than Granddad's.

Inside the ranch house, Granddad and Blue Sky went through the greeting ceremony with noisy pleasure. When it was over, Granddad began his daily chat with the bird.

"You know that new raven, don't you?" he asked. "Otherwise you would have nailed it. Is it a brother or sister? Don't answer. We'll find out. A DNA test will speak for you."

Granddad got to his feet and walked to the dining table. Blue Sky flew to his own chair back and then hopped onto his plate. Grandma Sally served the two of them, then herself and Singing Bird. When the meal was done, Granddad's medicine-taking ritual began. The medicine ritual went like this:

Every day Grandma Sally quietly put out the little dish of pills for Granddad. Blue Sky hopped to the dish and picked up the orange pill.

"NO!" Granddad shouted, and snatched the pill from Blue Sky's beak. "Want to kill yourself? That's what's the matter with me. Pills. They make me feel lousy." Grandma Sally then brought a glass of fresh-squeezed orange juice, and Granddad swallowed the pills.

He grimaced and looked out the window to see Charlie crossing the yard with the live trap. Granddad rose to get bait for it and sat down quickly.

"Sally," he said. "Give me a hand. I'm a little wobbly. It's that orange pill."

"Nonsense," she said. "You stay there. I'll get the bait." She looked out the window, then hurriedly opened the door.

"Charlie," she shouted. "Go close the cattle gate! Two bison are headed in."

"Chase them off," Granddad called happily. He enjoyed living among wild animals that considered all land was their land.

Charlie put down the live trap, splashed through the irrigation ditch, and reached the gate at the same time the bison did. They blinked and lowered their heads at him. Like a flash he was on the bottom board of the gate pushing it closed with one foot. He bolted it and shook his fist at the huge animals.

"Stay away from Granddad's trees," he yelled. "You've taken the bark off too many, rubbing them with your big heads and backs." He picked up the trap and went on to the ranch house.

Granddad baited it, set the trigger, and rested in his chair while Charlie took it up on the roof.

"And be careful of the wooden shingles," Grandma Sally called as she came out of the kitchen. "They're fragile." Charlie shinnied up the porch post and clambered onto the roof. Grandma Sally handed him the trap.

"Wow! Ouch!" he yelled. He hurriedly placed the trap where the ravens would have easy access to it and swung down to the porch. From the porch he dashed into the kitchen.

"What's the matter?" Singing Bird asked. "A raven bite you?"

"No, I got hit in the head with a pinecone."

"Write that down," said Granddad. "And add that the 'parents' of Blue Sky have attacked." His eyes twinkled.

"How do you know they're his parents?" Charlie asked.

"They are throwing pinecones at you. They recognize you as the person who took their nestling."

"They recognize me?" Charlie asked. "I sure don't recognize them as Blue Sky's parents."

"Just because *you* don't doesn't mean they are as limited as you are. I banded a male and female robin and their nestlings one spring when I was young. Every year after that when I passed near the robin nest, the male, yelled, dove, and wing-clipped me. He didn't dive at the postman or anyone else—just me. That bird never forgot me.

"You robbed the raven nest," he went on. "They know you well, and they have it in for you." Charlie rubbed his head and grinned.

"Then why don't they give the alarm cry when they see me?"

Granddad's eyes had that faraway look that dimmed them when he was searching for answers beyond the human mind.

"I don't know," he finally said. "Maybe it's because you're taking such good care of Blue Sky. Ravens are opportunists among other things. You're such a good source of food that they've brought their other offspring to you."

"I believe," said Grandma Sally, thinking back on her child-raising days, "that Blue Sky and the new bird are brother and sister and their parents brought the sister here to keep the two together. At least that is what I would have done."

"Brother and sister, or brother and brother or sister and sister, or just friends, who knows," said Granddad, being noncommittal. "We can't be sure until we send their DNA samples to the genetics lab and get a reply.

"But I think you're right." He winked at her.

Hardly had they gone indoors than they heard the sound of the trapdoor falling closed. The young raven visitor was caught. Charlie climbed up on the roof and brought down the cage and bird. In a few short moments Granddad had banded the new raven with both a blue and an aluminum band.

"I dub it Pinecone," said Singing Bird, looking at the welt on Charlie's forehead.

Granddad chuckled. He liked the name but didn't say so. He had other things on his mind.

"Charlie," he said. "Get a feather from both little ravens, label and date them, and Grandma will mail them to the lab. She knows where to send them after all these years of assisting me."

Promptly Grandma Sally put the labeled feathers in a sterile bag and then a mailer. She addressed it to the University of Idaho.

When the excitement was over, Granddad was ready to rest, but not before looking at his "Things to Do" calendar.

"Charlie," he said. "It's time to go to the National Forest and cut trees for the woodstove. Our permit's for today. Grandma will drive you. The ravens will keep me company.

"And, oh, call your mom and dad. They'll want to come too."

"I can't go," said Charlie. "I've got to go hunting food for Blue Sky and Pinecone."

"I'll do that," said Singing Bird. "Baby ravens eat so much they need two parents, and the roadkill should be good today. The summer tourists in Teton National Park are as thick as ants on a chocolate chip cookie. They never slow down for animals that cross the road. Maybe I'll even find a dead coyote. Some people actually try to hit them." She shivered.

Singing Bird thanked Sally for breakfast and went home to get her bike and to tell her parents that Charlie and his parents were going for wood. On Sagebrush Flats "going for wood" was a congenial phrase that meant, "let's all get together and help each other." Flying Cloud was pleased to hear the news.

"Tell them we can all go in my big truck," he said.

"And," said Soaring Swallow, "tell Sally I'll stay with Will. I know how much she loves to go to the forest for firewood."

The woodcutters did not get back until around four o'clock in the afternoon. As they turned into the yard, Singing Bird came to meet them on the run.

"Oh, I hope Will's all right," Grandma Sally said. Flying Cloud drove the truck slowly toward Granddad's porch and nearby woodshed. Charlie stuck his head out of the window and looked for Blue Sky.

"Guess what?" Singing Bird said, jumping on the running board. "When I got back from food hunting, I found Pinecone and Blue Sky playing together. I mean they played—they jumped over each other, rolled, chased, and played tag."

"Why, that's just like children," said Grandma Sally. "We should give them some Legos."

"I sort of did," Singing Bird said. "I didn't mean to. I took off my silver earrings because they were hurting and laid them on Charlie's steps. Blue Sky 'quorked,'—'Mine'— and flew off with one of them. He took it to the roof. He played with it. He never dropped it once. Then he hid it." She tilted her head and smiled with satisfaction.

"I'll climb up and get it for you," said Charlie.

"No, don't. Ravens love pretty things. He can have it. But that's not the big news. The big news is that just a few minutes ago the parents came and took Pinecone home. I watched them fly all the way back to the nest on Bison Butte."

"Goodness," said Grandma Sally. "The Bison Butte pair dropped off their child and picked it up when school was over? Looks like we really do have a Day Care Center." She pondered, and the wrinkles around her bright eyes creased playfully. "How sensible."

"We'll see if it happens again," said Charlie, taking Granddad's role of advocating data collecting. "Maybe it was just a once-in-a-lifetime thing."

Flying Cloud backed the truck up to the porch. When Charlie, Singing Bird, and her dad had stacked firewood on the porch and in the shed, they drove off to unload the rest of the wood in Flying Cloud's woodshed not far from the teepee.

Every day for a week Charlie wrote the same thing in his journal:

The raven parents dropped off Pinecone around 7 a.m. and flew to the river. They came back around 4:30 p.m., called to him/her, and took him/her home. On the last page of his notebook he wrote: *Grandma Sally is right. We have a Day Care Center and we are the babysitters! The environment (meaning* ravens*) is changing our lives.*

Charlie had to scrunch up his writing as he finished the last page of the journal, so the next morning he asked Granddad for a new one.

CHAPTER SEVEN

The People Students

The DNA test showed that Blue Sky and Pinecone were, indeed, brother and sister. It also revealed that Blue Sky was a male and Pinecone a female.

"We guessed right," said Charlie and rolled his eyes at Granddad who pretended not to hear. He didn't like to be accused of guessing.

One morning when the raven parents dropped off Pinecone at the Raven Day Care Center, Blue Sky tried to lure his sister into Granddad's house for breakfast. He called "gro, gro, gro" from Charlie's shoulder. Pinecone fluttered her wings like a hungry, begging fledgling but would not come down from the roof. Blue Sky "quorked" and flew to the woodpile, called her once more, then flew to Charlie's shoulder.

"Pinecone won't come into the house," he said to Blue Sky. "Your raven mom put her in the Day Care Center, and she's not going to leave until her mom tells her to."

Inside the house Blue Sky flew to Granddad, who praised him effusively. Then Blue Sky proceeded to praise himself in fancy postures and feather displays.

"Some ego," Granddad said.

After breakfast Granddad went to his desk and made

notes, then walked to his easy chair. Charlie exchanged glances with Grandma Sally. Granddad was walking steadily. He was not only better, but a lot better.

Blue Sky is curing Granddad, he wrote in his notebook that night, then erased it. *Not enough evidence for Granddad. I'll keep observing.*

A few days later at breakfast Charlie saw Blue Sky snatch the orange pill when Grandma Sally pushed the little plate of pills to Granddad.

"No!" Granddad shouted and took it from the raven. "It'll kill you! I detest 'em." Charlie laughed and suggested to Grandma Sally that she serve the pills another way.

The next day she blended the pills into Granddad's scrambled egg. When the little dish did not appear, Blue Sky lifted his feathers until he looked to be twice his size and flew to the kitchen counter. "ca,ca,ca,ca,ca!" he yelled in anger, threw open Grandma Sally's recipe box, and grabbed a card in his beak. In an instant he had it shredded in pieces.

"Blue Sky! NO!" Grandma Sally shouted. "Bad bird. Bad bird!" She shook her finger at him, and Charlie rolled his eyes at Granddad. The *B* word had been spoken.

"He's just being a raven, Sally" Granddad said. "He's not bad. You messed up his routine."

"Being a raven, nothing," Grandma Sally snapped. "In my world what Blue Sky did is bad! He destroyed property."

Charlie saw it was time to take Blue Sky outdoors and

reached with both hands to pick him up. In a black mood of pique, Blue Sky dodged Charlie and flew to the door. "KEK!" he screamed.

"I'm the enemy again," said Charlie, sighing.

"Or I am," said Grandma Sally.

"knock, knock, knock" sounded above the cabin. Charlie dashed outside to see who was giving the power call. The Bison Butte parents were on the roof, telling Pinecone they were still boss. She flattened her feathers to her body, and with her neck pulled in, she crouched in the obedient raven posture. Blue Sky did not join them. Charlie thought he did not want to be dominated by his parents. In Blue Sky's eyes he had all the power. He could sit at the table. He could hold his head higher than Granddad's and tell him how important he was by flashing his "ears" and puffing out his throat shackles. He was boss bird among this human flock. He wanted no more parental domination.

Full of his own importance, Blue Sky waited on the woodpile until his parents flew off, their wing feathers drumming out a rhythmical swoosh, swoosh, swoosh. They rolled and tumbled through the sky. To Charlie it looked like they were celebrating their freedom from child care, but he would never write *that* down.

When they were out of sight, Pinecone relaxed and stood up. Charlie suspected the wing swooshes were a message to the young ravens, but what? "Stay there until we come for you?" He went to his cabin and paged through the list of raven communications scientist Bernd Heinrich had compiled—anger, affection, hunger, curiosity, playfulness, fright, boldness, depression—none of them seemed to cover orders to the young. Remembering Granddad's advice, he stopped guessing and wrote down what he had heard and seen.

Singing Bird came through the leafy wall of willows and aspens along the irrigation ditch, carrying her rod and creel.

"Charlie, sit down on your steps with Blue Sky," she said. "I have a story to tell you."

"Now?" said Charlie. "We've got to hunt for raven food."

"Now," she said. "I have to practice to become a storyteller. This will be a health story."

"A health story?" Charlie sat down.

"Long, long ago," Singing Bird began, "a Teton Sioux girl wanted to learn how Raven cured people. If she could learn from Raven, then she too could cure the ill.

"She packed food and journeyed to the forest where Raven lived. For days she watched and listened. She saw no herbs. She saw no antler powder, but she also saw no sick ravens.

"Then she saw Raven sit on a tree limb facing into the sun. He lifted his feathers to expose his legs and feet to the sunlight. He opened his beak and eyes.

"'Why are you doing that?' asked the girl.

"'I have feathers all over my body, and the only way I can get vitamin D is through my feet, my eyes, and my mouth.'

"'Is that why there are no sick ravens?' she asked.

"Raven answered yes."

"Are you making this up?" Charlie was suddenly suspicious of the vitamin D knowledge. Singing Bird covered her laugh. "Yes," she answered. "I just read in *Science Discoveries* how birds get vitamin D and thought it would make a good story."

"It does."

"The problem with the old Teton Sioux legend that says ravens cure others," mused Singing Bird, "is that it doesn't tell how. Now I have a 'how' story."

"I thought just having a raven around cured," Charlie said. "Seems to be working in Granddad's case."

"Maybe," said Singing Bird.

"Time to go food hunting for Blue Sky and Pinecone," Charlie said, and got his collecting bag.

"Don't forget your fishing rod," Singing Bird added.

Blue Sky and Pinecone accompanied the two food gatherers, not on their shoulders, but by flying to a telephone pole, waiting for them to catch up, then flying on to the next. At Sagebrush Flats Road the foursome stopped to watch a group of ravens. The birds were diving and circling just uphill of the Spinders' log house. Several folded their wings and sped to earth.

"They're asking for it," Charlie said. "They are awfully close to the house, and they know Mr. Spinder is 'bad.'" He grinned.

"They don't seem to care," said Singing Bird. "They're flying so beautifully they look like ballet dancers."

"The Spinders must be away," said Charlie. "When the Spinders are outside, the ravens scream 'Enemy, enemy'— 'KEK,KEK,KEK,KEK.'"

"Maybe the Spinders are inside loading their guns," suggested Singing Bird.

"I sure hope not," said Charlie. "Let's fish off the bridge.

We can keep an eye on the ravens and the Spinders from there."

Charlie led her through the elderberry bushes and blue flax flowers, up onto the bridge, where they sat with their legs hanging over the edge. They dropped their lines into the water. Blue Sky and Pinecone perched in a cottonwood nearby and preened.

Charlie glanced at Bison Butte, looking for Blue Sky's parents. The butte rose almost straight up from the ravine the creek had cut. A raven called from the tree on the summit. After a few minutes a large flock of ravens appeared in the sky. They were strung out like pen marks against the white peaks of the Teton Mountains.

"They're sending a message in hieroglyphics," said Singing Bird.

"Looks like it, doesn't it?" said Charlie. "I think the writing says, 'beware the Spinders.'"

Suddenly a gunshot sounded. A raven screamed, "KEK, KEK,KEK,KEK,KEK,KEK," and the sky was suddenly empty of ravens. Even the tree swallows and mountain bluebirds knew the raven enemy alarm. They went into hiding. Blue Sky and Pinecone dropped down into the elderberry bushes and stood still. They also knew what to do.

After a moment Charlie climbed onto the bridge railing to see what had been killed. "They missed."

"How do you know?"

"No black feathers floating on the air, and the resident ravens aren't moaning for the dead."

"Ravens know about death?" asked Singing Bird.

"Every animal does, especially ravens and crows. Grand-dad kept crows from his corn crop when he was a boy by hanging a dead crow on a post in the field. They saw it, moaned, and never came back."

A horse neighed. Voices called out. Charlie glanced toward the Spinders' ranch house. As if possessed by spirits Mr. and Mrs. Spinder galloped their Appaloosas through the gate and east toward Morton. Charlie glowered at them.

"What we need," he said emphatically, "is a dead raven to put on Mr. Spinder's roof. It'll drive the ravens away from Mr. Spinder and his gun."

"Best idea," Singing Bird answered. "We'll get one"

"Don't even think what you're thinking," Charlie said.

"I'm not thinking that. You are. I'm thinking Dad's got a lot of raven feathers he decorates head bonnets with. Flying Cloud and I will make a dead raven."

"That's terrific."

Charlie's line suddenly jerked, and he reeled in and landed a good-size fish. After Singing Bird caught one, they decided they had enough food for the young ravens and started home. Halfway up the embankment to the county road, Singing Bird found a dead woodchuck.

"Either a car or a coyote did this," she said. "But wow, we have food for days." They trotted down the side of the road.

"Wait a second," Charlie said and stopped. "I've just had a raven thought."

"What's a raven thought?"

"Mysterious."

"Now what?"

"The ballet of ravens dropped down onto one spot for some raven reason. And some of them haven't left. I'm going there."

"So am I," said Singing Bird, and they waded back across the stream, pushed through the elderberry bushes, and climbed almost to the pine forest. Blue Sky and Pinecone did not follow them. They were on their way home; and home to the ranch house they went.

A sentinel raven saw Charlie and Singing Bird when they were still a good distance away. He gave no alarm cry but sent his message by flying quietly away. Ten or twelve more ravens got his message and left in silence. Charlie hurried across swatches of pink gentian and blue lupine flowers to the gathering spot. There lay the carcass of a mule deer. A weasel and a coyote that had been feeding on the carcass with the ravens ran into the woods. Crows departed. A bald eagle saw them, hopped onto a thermal—a rising body of warm air—and spiraled skyward with it.

"Cool," Charlie said, pointing to the retreating feasters. "Ravens share their food."

"That makes them good," Singing Bird said. "Write that down."

When the two got home Blue Sky and Pinecone were already there, napping in the cool of Charlie's cabin. Grandma Sally was stacking wood near the porch door, where it could be easily reached when the snows came.

"How's Granddad?" Charlie asked her.

"Not good," she said. "He's just had a setback. He's upset, and that's not good for him." She wiped the perspiration from her sunburned face and tapped the logs with a mallet to jar them into settling firmly. "I hate to tell you this, Charlie, but Blue Sky and his sister put holes in one of the river rafts and let all the air out. Granddad got very agitated. The raft is ruined. Your dad called, and he thinks it's time you set Blue Sky free."

"But he IS free!"

"Oh, I know, I know," said Grandma Sally. "I don't like to be like this. I really love that bird, but I do worry about Granddad so. Those rafts are very expensive, and the thought of replacing one depressed him so much, he slumped back in his chair, drooped his head, and hasn't spoken since." She picked up another piece of firewood. "Maybe your dad would drive the birds to Yellowstone Park and set them free."

Charlie couldn't believe his ears.

"No, no, please don't. Besides, Blue Sky will come right back. I'm his mother—or"—he paused and looked at his cabin where the little ravens slept—"if he doesn't, he'll die. The resident ravens will attack him."

Grandma Sally put her arm around Charlie.

"I'm sorry," she said. "There are some days when Blue Sky really does make your granddad better. And then there are days like this."

"There must be a reason for the ups and downs," said Singing Bird.

"There must be," said Grandma Sally, "and we best keep Blue Sky around until we know."

She squeezed Charlie's shoulder. "I love that crazy bird too."

"Well, then," said Charlie, "I'd better feed him." He carried the fish and woodchuck to the fish cleaning table and cut them into small pieces for the birds.

"You know, Charlie," Singing Bird said as she scaled a fish, "you need three columns in your study—Good, Bad, and Mysterious. Why would Blue Sky attack a raft? He must know it's no enemy."

"I don't know," he said. "The raft doesn't shoot ravens. Yep, you're right, I need a Mysterious column."

"And," said Singing Bird, "the first entry is: 'Pecks holes in rafts.'"

"That also goes in the Bad column," Charlie mused. He scratched his head. "I wonder why he did it? He can't eat rafts."

When the raven food was stored in the freezer and Charlie and Singing Bird had washed up, Singing Bird picked up her rod and creel.

"I'm going home to make a false dead raven," she said and took the trail through the willows. It, like the bison trails on the sagebrush flats, had been made by the comings and goings of feet—hers and Charlie's.

The door burst open and Granddad came out on the porch. He seemed to be full of energy.

"Move the carcass, Charlie! You've got to move the carcass!" He shook his cane. "I've been watching that kettle of ravens over there by the Spinders. They're on a carcass. Go move it before that man thinks devils are in his backyard and shoots them." He teetered. Grandma Sally ran to steady him, and Charlie jumped up all three steps in one leap and took his arm. Granddad pushed them both away. "Let go," he said. "I'm fine." But he sat down on the steps.

Charlie sat down beside him. "Singing Bird has a good idea," he said. "She's going to make a false dead raven to scare the ravens away from Mr. Spinder's ranch."

"Now that's intelligent," Granddad said.

"Write it down!"

"I will," said Charlie.

"Write it down!"

"I will, Granddad, I will!" Charlie said impatiently.

Granddad looked at him. "That wasn't me, saying 'write it down,'" he said.

"It wasn't?" Charlie's eyes widened. "It sounded like you." They stared at each other as they slowly realized that the unimaginable was happening.

"Write it down!" came a voice from above. Blue Sky looked over the edge of the roof.

"Write it down!" he repeated.

"Granddad!" Charlie rubbed his chin. "We have an English-speaking raven." Granddad laughed at the wonder of it all. Grandma Sally's facial expression was not to be fathomed.

"What are you thinking?" Granddad asked her.

"That I'm grateful he didn't say, 'Nevermore.'"

"He may yet," said Granddad, getting to his feet. "This is turning out to be quite a convoluted study. The raven is studying us." He hobbled off into the house.

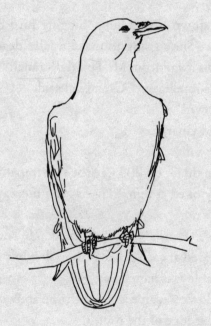

CHAPTER EIGHT

Independence Day

No sooner had Charlie gone off to his cabin to write notes than Granddad reappeared outside. He had small pieces of venison in his hand. He clicked his tongue to imitate the "knock trill" food call of the adult raven.

"Write it down!" said Blue Sky, and flew to his shoulder.

"I will," said Granddad, feeding him and expressing his affection by "kmmmm gurgling." "You're one cute bird," he concluded in English. Charlie heard the man-to-bird talk and came outside.

"What are you doing here, Granddad?" he asked. "You should be resting."

"I've just rewarded Blue Sky for his people talk. There is nothing like a reward to make even a raven remember his lesson."

Charlie ushered Granddad back indoors to his chair and sat down on the stool beside him. Granddad was pale, raven or no raven. Charlie picked up a book and read aloud until the old naturalist fell asleep.

And while he read, the clock hands swung to 4 P.M.

Pinecone sat on the roof, waiting for her parents to take her home. They did not. At 5 P.M., when they still had not appeared, she drooped her head and wings.

After a long slump, Pinecone hopped to the rain gutters, flew to the foot of Charlie's cabin steps, and feathers flattened to her body in fear, walked under a clump of flowering yampas. She pulled in her neck and made herself small. A white-crowned sparrow in the willow overhead fed her tiny nestlings. Pinecone opened her mouth to be fed. Nothing happened. She closed it.

After dinner Charlie returned to his cabin to write down all he had seen. Then the sun went down behind the mountain peaks. The afterglow colored the mountains and valley red-orange, and abandoned Pinecone stepped out from under the yampa plant. Hesitatingly she hopped up the cabin steps, peeked in the open door, and went in. Blue Sky flew down from the back of Charlie's chair and greeted her.

Charlie wrote:

June 30. Blue Sky talks. He says, "Write it down." Mysterious? Supernatural? Or is he just being a raven like Edgar Allan Poe's? That's a great poem. I reread it.

A rustle of wings. Charlie turned around. Blue Sky and Pinecone were sitting at the foot of his bed.

Big news, he wrote. *Pinecone is spending the night. It must be because her parents didn't come for her. That means today is independence day for her—and for her brother too. And that could be why he poked holes in the raft. Is he looking for a new source of food now that he is on his own? If that's it, he must sense that I, like his parents, will no longer feed him—that's a guess. All I should write down is that he let the air out of the raft—and Grandma Sally was mad. Those are the true facts.*

Charlie wrote on:

I'm not supposed to guess, but I can't help it. My guess is that raven independence day is also why Blue Sky talked. He's experimenting with clever ways to get food. Talking worked. Smart bird.

Hours later a full moon rose over Goat Mountain and swathed the valley in a silver light so bright a sandhill crane standing on one leg in the irrigation ditch saw a frog and caught it.

Charlie was awakened by Singing Bird tapping on his window.

"Charlie, wake up. It's me." He rolled out of his sleeping bag completely dressed. That was another joy of having his own cabin. He could go to bed with his clothes on if he wanted to. He opened the door.

"What's up?" he asked.

"Look!" Charlie saw a dead raven.

"Wow, what did you do? You didn't kill a raven, did you?" He scrambled for a match and lit his kerosene lamp.

"Of course not," she snapped. "That's an insult. You know I would never do that. I made a dead raven." She brought it closer to the lamp.

"It sure looks real," Charlie exclaimed. "Big beak and all. It's great!"

"Dad says we should put it on Mr. Spinder's roof tonight. He and his wife have gone to a hunting club in Pinedale to practice for the elk-hunting season. They won't be back for three days. They asked Dad to feed their horses."

Blue Sky and Pinecone shook their feathers to say they were being disturbed.

Charlie pulled on his parka to fend off the cold night air of the mountain valley, slipped into his boots, and headed out for the Spinders with Singing Bird. The moonlit flats were a busy place. Near the butte a family of mule deer grazed, and two great horned owl youngsters called for food. A pack of coyotes howled. They were answered by another family far out in the sagebrush. And then a wolf howled.

"A wolf," said Charlie. "Hey! The wolves that were reintroduced to Yellowstone Park have come down to our valley. The park naturalist said they would and told us to watch for them."

"What a beautiful sound," said Singing Bird.

"Now we are whole again," said Charlie. "The wolves have returned."

As they approached the Spinders' ranch they stopped talking. Charlie quietly unfastened the gate and opened it a crack. He and Singing Bird slipped through, trying not to disturb the Appaloosas. The horses had keen ears, and even a rolling pebble could make them whinny and stamp their hoofs.

When they were a short distance away from the ranch house, Charlie whispered, "Stay here. I'll be right back." Singing Bird sat down on a log and clasped her knees.

"Raven Owners, Raven Owners," she chanted to herself. "Please keep the Spinders in Pinedale." She hadn't mentioned to Charlie that Flying Cloud had told her the Spinders said they were going to be gone for three days but had left only enough horse food for one.

Suddenly the false dead raven rose out of the shadows, soared up and up and plopped down on the roof of the house. It fluttered, the feathers whooshing, and lay still. Charlie came back.

"Let's go," he said and led the way to the road. "We'll hide in the sagebrush out on the flat and see what happens."

"I'm going home," Singing Bird said. "The sun and the ravens won't be up for five hours and I'm sleepy. Besides, if I'm not home soon my father will be so worried he'll be here on the wind and calling so loudly he'll avalanche the rocks on the mountains."

Charlie watched Singing Bird until she faded into the moonlight. She might have been one of her ancestors walking home through this unchanged landscape, listening to the unchanged voices of wolf and owl.

When he could no longer see her, Charlie tucked his

parka under his head, lay back, and watched the stars. They grew brighter as the moon went down and paler as the sun came up.

A truck turned onto Sagebrush Flats Road and stopped at the Spinders' gate. Charlie rolled to all fours. Mr. Spinder and another man jumped from the cab and opened it. The truck rolled into the blue predawn shadows of the cotton-woods that surrounded the Spinder ranch house and the motor was turned off. No lights came on in the house.

Why not? He waited and waited. Where were the people? Charlie decided he must know what they were do-ing. He crossed the road to Cache Creek and worked his way up the noisy stream until he saw Mr. and Mrs. Spinder and their visitor. They were erecting a mist net behind the deer carcass. It is a fine, almost transparent netting that birds can't see. They fly into it and get caught, but not harmed. Naturalists like his granddad use them to catch birds. Then they band and set them free, so they can study them.

Charlie didn't think Mr. Spinder had any such plan in mind. In fact, this was a good way for Mr. Spinder to get rid of lots of ravens silently. Grandma Sally had told him that ravens were protected, and he didn't want to get caught shooting them. But if he killed them quietly no one would know and he wouldn't go to jail.

Charlie was alarmed by this new twist in what now seemed to be a war between Mr. Spinder and the ravens. He watched from behind a tree. The Spinders and the visitor finished setting up the mist net and went down through the trees and into the ranch house. The lights came on.

Now what do I do? Charlie asked himself. Should I tear down the net? Vandalism. I don't have time to get the sheriff. While Charlie was pondering, the sun came up.

The sky brightened. A lone raven, a scout, came over Bison Butte. He flew as swiftly as a Sioux arrow. He climbed high then began circling. Three more ravens joined him. The three folded their wings and dropped straight down toward the carcass. Charlie held his breath. They were going to be caught and then killed.

The scout kept circling above the Spinder ranch house.

"KEK,KEK,KEK,KEK,KEK,KEK." The alarm cry of the raven shattered the air.

And all the ravens were gone.

Charlie went whistling home. Singing Bird was a heroine, and her false dead raven a masterpiece of success. He jumped and clicked his heels together.

CHAPTER NINE

Other Raven Speak

As the summer days grew shorter the flowers of the bull thistles cast a purple haze across the flats, and enrollment at the Day Care Center grew.

Charlie knew why. Pinecone and Bernd Heinrich's book had given him the answer. When raven parents suddenly stop feeding their youngsters they drive them off their properties. Being social animals they hang out together—the more eyes and ears, the easier to find food and spot enemies. Granddad's roof provided the food and it was high above the coyotes and safe from automobiles.

August 5, Charlie wrote. *Four more young ravens have joined the Center on Granddad's roof. They come and go all day. Three now spend the night in that blue spruce that grows near the pump house. That makes them our very own ravens—our residents.*

The next day, while Charlie was splitting wood for kindling, he saw one of the members of the Day Care Center leave the roof and fly across the sagebrush toward Bison Butte. Charlie climbed the cottonwood to see how far he would get before the parent ravens drove him off.

Over the Spinders' ranch house the bird called, "KEK,KEK,KEK,KEK," pulled down one wing, and made a right turn. He sped off toward the river. But no adult birds pursued him. Charlie grinned. He knew what had happened. The youngster had gotten as far as the Spinders' ranch house where it had seen Singing Bird's false dead raven and fled. It was still sending out its message of death. The Day Care ravens were still safe from mist nets and guns.

Suddenly one day Blue Sky changed his routine again. He didn't come to breakfast with Granddad. Instead he ate with his friends on the roof. Charlie noted that and added:

Eating with his friends is Blue Sky's choice, so he isn't mad and sulky like he is when I change his routine. Ravens like to make up their own minds.

Granddad was especially disappointed not to have him at the breakfast table.

"For some reason," he mused, "when Blue Sky doesn't come to breakfast I don't feel well all that day."

"That's not good," said Charlie. "I'm putting his absence in the Bad column." Then he thought about it and changed his mind.

"No," he said, "it goes under Mysterious."

Granddad ate lunch in his chair that day. Charlie helped him cut up his meat. "I saw something interesting this morning," he said. "Two members of the Day Care Center were perched side by side and one was holding the other's beak."

"They sound like an item to me," said Granddad. "They're too young to mate, but maybe they're telling us that ravens choose mates when they're kids—like I did." He glanced up to wink at Sally, but she was outside weeding the lettuce.

"One of the pair has a missing tail feather," Charlie said. "We can recognize him by that and see if he really has picked her as a mate." Granddad nodded and made an attempt to get up, but he slumped back in his chair.

"Keep me informed," he said in a tired voice. "I'll observe from the window." Blue Sky had not come to breakfast. Granddad took out his little black book and wrote: *I really don't feel as well when Blue Sky skips breakfast with me!*

Suddenly Grandma Sally banged the front door open and rushed in the house.

"Oh, Charlie." She sighed, clasping her hands tightly. "The worst has happened."

Charlie felt a cold shock go down his spine. Granddad awoke from his torpor.

"What happened?" he shouted. "Tell us!"

"Blue Sky walked behind me in the garden," she said. "I thought how cute, and then I turned around. He had yanked up all the lettuce and shredded it to bits." She walked into the living room. "I was planning our own, very own mountain-grown salad for tomorrow," she said and sank down on a chair. "I am so mad . . ." She walked to the window. "I could shake him until all his feathers fly off!"

Charlie and Granddad looked at each other. They did not say what they had thought the "worst" was—that Mr. Spinder had shot Blue Sky. But they also did not say, Thank goodness it was only the lettuce. That bright green garden of lettuce was Grandma Sally's fight with the short summer season.

Grandma Sally turned from the window and patted Granddad's shoulder. "It's okay," she said. "I'll try again next year. . . . And I do like Blue Sky—a lot." Granddad took her hand in his and squeezed it tenderly.

Much to Granddad's delight, the next morning Blue Sky changed his mind again and rode into the ranch house on Charlie's shoulder. They performed the greeting ceremony as well as the breakfast and medicine ritual. Then, as was his habit, Blue Sky walked to the door to be let out.

When he was gone, Granddad asked Charlie to set up the

spotting scope at the big window so he could watch the ravens.

"Well, Blue Sky's back with me at breakfast, and I feel pretty good," he said. "Thank goodness. There is so much raven activity to watch now."

"Why is that?" Charlie asked.

"Winter is coming. They're gearing up for change."

While they were adjusting the scope, Missing Feather flew by, chasing a mouse. He pursued it out of the yard and into the sagebrush. His friend—Granddad had dubbed her, Miss Item—dropped from the roof and landed on a squirming nest of young mice. Missing Feather looped back and shared the morsels.

"Gee," said Charlie. "Ravens hunt like coyotes. They work together in teams. Missing Feather chased the adult away from the nest and Miss Item closed in on the young. Then she and her friend shared the food. I'd better write down that ravens are coyotes."

"And add," said Granddad, peering through the spotting scope, "that we've got the sexes wrong. Missing Feather just accepted a tasty mouse from Miss Item—as female ravens do, not males."

"Well," said Charlie. "It's a good thing *they* know who they are."

That afternoon the three members of the Day Care Center who roosted in the trees took off from the roof, spread their wings, and flew toward the river in sight of Granddad's scope. They flew side by side, gamboling and tumbling in the air. They performed swan dives and backflips. With the sunlight flashing on their wings, they shot like missiles into the trees along the Snake River.

"Now that was good medicine," said Granddad, and he walked to the kitchen for a glass of water.

That evening, only two of the three young ravens returned from the river at dusk. Knocking and quorking, they glided to their roost in Granddad's trees.

Grandma Sally was on the porch getting a slingful of wood for the fire when they came home. They were drooping their wings and moaning. She finished loading the sling and hurried indoors.

"Will," she said, "two of the overnight ravens are acting as if they are miserable. They moan and droop their wings, and their little hearts pounded so hard I could see their feathers jump."

"How many, did you say?"

"Two."

"One of our three is missing."

"What does that mean?"

"By the way you describe their behavior, their companion met its death."

"Oh, no," said Grandma Sally. "I want them all to live."

"This is the hard part of being a human in a study like this," said Granddad. "The mortality rate of young wild things is very, very high—sixty percent never make it." Grandma Sally turned abruptly away and opened the wooden box that held the matches.

"Will," she called out rather sharply. "What is your orange pill doing behind the matchbox? You didn't take it today, did you? You hid it."

"I hate those pills," he said. "I feel worse after I take them."

Scolding, clucking, and shaking her head, Grandma Sally brought him the pill with a glass of water.

"Call the undertaker," he said and swallowed it.

In the morning Blue Sky again rode on Charlie's shoulder to greet and have breakfast with Granddad. Pinecone flew to the roof. She still could not make the transition from mere friendship with people to the intimacy that Blue Sky enjoyed with them. But she did have some raven feelings for them. She followed any member of the human family who came outdoors and kept a curious eye on the goings-on inside the house by sitting on the woodpile and looking through the window.

This morning the Granddad-greeting ritual went well. Then the pill dish came out. Blue Sky yelled, "Write it down!" and snatched the orange pill. Granddad reached for him. Grandma Sally gave Granddad his juice and threw Blue Sky out the door. He seemed to like the sensation of being picked up and tossed in the air and let himself be catapulted into space. He then spread his wings and coasted to the roof of Charlie's cabin.

Several days went by.

August 8, Charlie wrote. *This morning I heard Blue Sky yelling, "Write it down," and found him in the pine tree* beside the pump house. On the limb not far from him was a young porcupine. Seems that "Write it down" gets Blue Sky attention. That's good, but Grandma Sally is not going to like having porcupines in her yard. Last year a porcupine ate the kitchen windowsill and the handle of her axe.

What to do. First of all, I must get Blue Sky away from the beast before he sticks him with quills. Then I have to put any tools that have salt from the sweat of hands on them in the basement.

To get Blue Sky away from the porcupine, I lured him to my shoulder with a piece of jerky. He carried it to the roof. Since he had just eaten I knew he would want to hide it, but not while the members of the Day Care Center were watching. I have noticed that he never hides food when other ravens are there. And they don't hide food when he is watching. I don't think they trust one another.

Finally, when all the birds were off foraging, Blue Sky hid the jerky under a shingle. Birds can't smell well, so it's safe.

August 9. But porcupines can smell!

Last night when Blue Sky was asleep, Quills climbed up onto the roof, found the jerky, and ate it along with half of two salty shingles.

Grandma Sally, wrote Charlie, will give Blue Sky a "Bad" mark for hiding the jerky on the roof, where it would flavor the shingles. And I'll get a bad mark too. I *shouldn't have given Blue Sky that jerky when he had just finished breakfast.*

I guess I'll have to confess to Grandma Sally, then replace the shingles and let her know a porcupine has joined the Day Care Center.

The next morning, when Charlie was on his way to breakfast, Blue Sky rode on his head. He cocked an ear skyward to listen, drew his feathers to his body, and took off.

"KEK, KEK, KEK, KEK."

The last two overnight members of the Day Care Center heard the alarm and flew away without a sound. In the silence that settled over the songbirds and little mammals, Charlie heard the rhythmical beat of a horse trot, and Mr. Spinder rode up to the gate. Charlie again wondered what the man had done to make the ravens fear him so. Nevertheless he welcomed Mr. Spinder with a "Howdy."

"How's your granddad?" the neighbor asked.

Charlie couldn't resist. "He's better. A raven's curing him."

Mr. Spinder's eyes narrowed.

"Killing him, you mean." He stuck his thumbs in his pant pockets. "Is your grandmother here? I'd like to speak to her." He seemed upset, so Charlie quickly opened the door. Granddad was in his chair, looking through the spotting scope. Grandma Sally was in the kitchen, preparing dog chow and canned cat food for the Day Care Center—mounds of it. There were still about six young ravens that came to the center for "milk and crackers."

She was surprised to see Mr. Spinder. He had not been around since she had told him it was illegal to kill ravens.

"We are being spied on," Mr. Spinder said and walked right past her to Granddad.

"Oh, nonsense," said Grandma Sally, joining them. "Who would want to spy on us?"

"Spirits of the dead."

"Is that so?" commented Granddad.

"Yes, and they talk."

"Spirits talk? That's pretty unusual."

"It's either spirits or the FBI is spying on me. I say it's spirits because no one's there."

"Out there a lot of things sound like people talking," said Granddad. "I have been fooled by a murmuring stream. And coyotes and wind and even baby birds."

"The words I hear," Mr. Spinder said, "are as clear as your voice."

Charlie, who was listening in the doorway, joined them.

"What are the words?" asked Granddad.

"'Write it down. Write it down.' And there is no one there. I've looked, circled the house, the barn—watched the road. No one. The devil or the FBI is spying on me—keeping notes."

"Have you done anything wrong?" asked Granddad.

"I'm very serious," Mr. Spinder snorted. "In case you don't know it, ravens are a curse." He looked at Granddad. "And I am trying to save you."

"How are you doing that?" asked Grandma Sally.

"Shooting them."

Charlie's mouth dropped open. So that's why the ravens called Mr. Spinder an enemy. He did shoot them. He did.

"But that didn't work," Mr. Spinder went on. "More and more arrived. They gathered on a carcass uphill of me. So I erected a net to trap and kill them—for your sake. But they didn't come near the net. They flew over my house, yelled, and went away. Then an elk walked through the net and that was that."

"You're better off," said Charlie. "It's illegal to kill ravens."

"But ravens bring death," Mr. Spinder said. "We must get rid of them. I see them on your property."

Granddad did not say more. Mr. Spinder just could not be rational on this subject. The man feared ravens the way many people fear snakes.

"Then who is speaking to me?" Mr. Spinder went on. "Who is saying, 'Write it down'? I'm not crazy. Mrs. Spinder hears the voice too."

"My pet raven," Charlie finally said, although he was aware that Mr. Spinder probably knew that "pet" made a creature an easy target for his gun. "Ravens and crows, like parrots and mynah birds and even starlings, can imitate human speech."

"Pet raven? You have made a pet of a raven?" Mr. Spinder sat down and held his head. Then without saying another word he got to his feet, walked outside, and mounted his horse. He was worried.

Granddad took out his notebook and wrote a few words.

"What did you write?" Charlie asked, fearing that he too thought Mr. Spinder might shoot Blue Sky.

"That I must talk to Mr. Spinder," he answered. "Knowledge can set him free."

"Tell him about the ravens in the Tower of London," Grandma Sally said. "They're good and also beloved. Charles II kept them in the tower because a soothsayer told him disaster would befall the city if they left. Generations of ravens have been there ever since. You can visit them today all these centuries later. They have guards to protect them—men in handsome red uniforms with black hats, Beefeaters they're called."

Granddad walked to the bookcase and took out a bird book, checked something, and put it back. Grandma and Charlie glanced at each other, amazed at how strong Granddad was today.

"Hey, Granddad," Charlie said. "Maybe there *is* raven magic. Look at you, you're walking perfectly. You really are better."

"Blue Sky and I have a secret."

He winked.

"Oh, for goodness' sakes," said Grandma Sally.

CHAPTER TEN

Messages from the Earth

After making a toasty fire in the woodstove to protect Granddad from the late-August chill, Charlie and Singing Bird set out on their bikes to find roadkill along the busy highway to Yellowstone Park. At a bend where the highway ran close to the Snake River they stopped. Two fledgling ospreys sat in a tree spotted with red autumn leaves. A bull elk bugled.

"Oh, no," said Charlie. "See those leaves? Hear that call? Summer's over up here in the mountains. Makes me sad."

"Me too," Singing Bird said. "Your school starts next week and mine in October."

"Don't remind me. I have to go back to town . . ."

". . . and leave Blue Sky," finished Singing Bird.

"Yeah," he said, "and leave Blue Sky. What'll he do for food?"

"He'll be fine," she said. "Blue Sky's independent now. He doesn't need your food . . . and besides, ravens live around these mountains all winter."

"Granddad said those are adults. The young like Blue Sky are driven away by adults."

"Does your granddad know where they go?"

"Not really," Charlie said. "That was his big study. The one he never finished. He put tiny radios on the immature ravens and followed their travels with receivers."

"What did he find out?"

"Not much. He had radios on three of them two years ago. One went to Bison Butte and was shot. The second joined a flock of young ravens in Teton National Park and a car hit her."

"The third?"

"The third just—vanished. She flew out of range of the receivers. Then Granddad got sick and the experiment stopped."

"Maybe you can go on with the study," Singing Bird said. "Blue Sky is banded. You can watch him this winter and see where he goes."

"That would be great," Charlie said. "But I'll be in town all week, and weekends aren't enough time."

Singing Bird shifted the road-killed muskrat in her basket, then pushed slowly down on her bike pedal and moved on. Charlie walked his bike. As they gathered to migrate south, tree swallows circled overhead like leaves in a whirlwind. The valley trees and grasses were shifting into their golden colors of autumn. Charlie paid them no attention.

"My real worry," he said, "is how to feed Blue Sky when I am in Jackson all week. He still can't tear up his food in pieces small enough to swallow."

"Grandma Sally could do that," Singing Bird said.

"Granddad won't let her. That's interfering with results. He's now telling me to stop feeding and babying Blue Sky. Says he must fend for himself."

"But, you've got to keep Blue Sky with Granddad," Singing Bird said. "He's curing him. He really is."

"He was," said Charlie. "Then Blue Sky stopped coming to visit him. He leaves my cabin just after sunup and doesn't come back until dusk. And Granddad is worse."

"Hmmm," said Singing Bird.

"It's really mysterious," said Charlie.

"What do you mean? What do you mean, 'mysterious'?"

"Well, when Blue Sky came in to breakfast, Granddad felt fine all day—walked around, went over his notes, even chatted on the phone with his friends. When Blue Sky didn't come to breakfast, Granddad didn't feel so well. This hasn't happened only recently. This was true all summer. I looked over my notes last night and Granddad was better on the days that Blue Sky came to breakfast—definitely."

"That's not good," Singing Bird said. "That proves he won't get better without a raven. We'll have to catch Blue Sky and keep him indoors with Granddad."

"I doubt if I can catch him," Charlie said. "He doesn't let me get my hands on him anymore. He'll sit on my shoulder and walk beside me, but when I try to pick him up—poof—he's out of reach. He reads me—knows what I'm doing before I do it."

Singing Bird pondered.

"Where does he go when he leaves for the day?" she finally asked. "Can we livetrap him there?"

"He heads out for the vast, vast sagebrush flats."

"Why? Does he catch food there?"

"I guess," said Charlie. "Maybe little stuff—grasshoppers, beetles, even mice. But he can't get much to eat because he can't tear up the carcasses of big animals, and he needs meat—lots of it. Maybe I have spoiled him. He still needs me to chop up his food."

"I can do that for a little while," Singing Bird said. "We don't leave for Standing Rock until October. Well, maybe a little earlier. Dad wants to take pictures of Standing Rock teepees for his book when the cottonwoods are bright yellow."

"Then when you're gone," said Charlie slowly, "the only ones left to chop up food for Blue Sky are the Spinders." They looked at each other and laughed.

While they were walking, a young wolf came out of the dense yellow rabbitbrush that grew on the other side of the highway and crossed to their side. Charlie saw her when she stopped. She glanced at the sky.

"A wolf," he whispered. "Oh, wow!" His heart beat faster. "That's the first one I've ever seen." He crouched in the sagebrush and pulled Singing Bird down with him.

"Must be one down from Yellowstone," she said.

"Yeah. Nice!"

The wolf flicked her ears nervously at the sound of their

whispers, but living in a national park where people could not hunt, she was not alarmed. Something in the sky held her rapt attention. Charlie and Singing Bird sat stone still and looked where she was looking. They saw nothing but clouds. Then a raven appeared from a great height and plunged earthward. It coasted to a landing a little distance in front of the wolf. The bird emitted several "boing" sounds then walked slowly forward. The wolf followed the raven.

When the raven checked to see if the wolf was behind him, the wolf playfully pounced and nipped its tail.

"They act like friends," said Charlie. "Talk about mysterious."

"Sshhhh," whispered Singing Bird.

The raven took to its wings and landed not fifteen feet from them. It gave three undulating territorial quorks.

It's saying it lives here, Charlie thought and wondered if it might be one of the Day Care Center members or, more likely, one of Blue Sky's parents. They owned tens of miles around Granddad's ranch, and he and Singing Bird were less than a mile from the house as the raven flies. Charlie took out his notebook and made a note of this.

Suddenly the raven in the sagebrush took off, flew a few feet above the vegetation, and wing-dipped. It pointed one wing down and pulled the other close to its body. As it did so, Charlie saw a red and an aluminum band on its right leg.

"Blue Sky!" He gestured to Singing Bird by pointing to the sky.

Blue Sky skimmed above the sagebrush, giving the food call, a knock and trill. The wolf crouched on her belly. Blue Sky wing-dipped again, his right wing looking like a finger pointing at something on the ground. The wolf went there and found a dead badger. She tore it into pieces and gulped down chunks. Blue Sky flew down and picked up and ate the small scattered pieces. The wolf did not bother the raven. The young raven was not afraid of the wolf.

"Looks like Blue Sky has solved my problem," said Charlie. "He has a wolf to tear up his food." He took out his notebook and began his writing with an exclamation point:

!I have seen a wolf, a beautiful wolf, and I have seen it do an extraordinary thing. It has torn up food that Blue Sky found and they both have eaten. WOW.

When Charlie was done with note taking, he and Singing Bird picked up their bikes.

"Want to know why Blue Sky has a wolf for a friend?" Singing Bird asked. "There's an old Teton Sioux story about this."

"Tell me," said Charlie.

As they walked homeward pushing their bikes, Singing Bird's jacket hit the wheel spokes like a drum beating time to her words.

"A long time ago," she said, "before there were people, a very lazy wolf was forced out of his den by his wife. She was hungry and the children were crying. 'Do not come back until you have food for us.' She bit his tail—hard—and he departed.

"Lazy Wolf walked and walked but saw nothing to eat, not even a mouse. At last he was tired and lay down.

"'I want to go home,' he cried, 'but I can't. I'll be bitten by my wife.' He threw back his head and howled.

"Raven appeared in the sky. He flew a short distance and cried, 'boing,' then tipped his wing.

"'Raven,' Wolf called, 'are you beckoning to me?' Raven tipped his wing again. Slowly Wolf got to his feet and climbed up and over a hill, following Raven. There before him lay a dead bison. Raven watched Wolf tear open the bison, then Raven "quorked" and announced the feast. The animals came: the weasel, the grizzly, the coyote, the fox, the wolverine, crows, eagles, magpies, beetles, and flies, and of course, the ravens.

"Wolf put the choice meat in his pack and was ready to go home. But before he departed he gave some of the best pieces to Raven and thanked him.

"Ever since that day Raven and Wolf have helped each other. Raven finds food and Wolf tears it open. On other occasions Raven follows Wolf until he kills food. Then Raven tells the whole community to come to the feast and shows them where it is by circling above it."

"We just saw that story happen," exclaimed Charlie.

"Let's find out if it's for real," Singing Bird said and took the muskrat out of her bike basket. Its hide had not been

damaged. A raven would need a predator to open it. She carried it into the sagebrush.

From his lookout high in the sky, Blue Sky saw her throw down the carcass, then hide with Charlie in the rabbitbrush. Blue Sky "boinged," but the wolf did not return. All three waited. No wolf.

"We might as well go," said Charlie. "Blue Sky's not telling the wolf where the muskrat is. If you can't repeat an experiment then it's not a truth."

But Blue Sky did not give up. He perched on a sagebrush stump near the muskrat. He listened, and looked, then flew away. Halfway across the flats he shot up in a spiral and called, "Boing, trilllll." He dove toward Singing Bird and Charlie. Above the muskrat he wing-tipped, and out of the sagebrush dashed the wolf. She pounced on the carcass.

"Write that down," Singing Bird said. "Ravens lead wolves to carcasses. Wolves open them and they both eat." They high-fived.

"We may not find out where Blue Sky goes in winter," said Charlie, "but Wolf will chop up his food for him." He was greatly relieved. "Let's go home."

When they reached Granddad's ranch house, the last member of the Resident Day Care Center returned to the trees for the night. But not Blue Sky or Pinecone. This was the first time that Charlie's beloved raven had not come home and brought Pinecone. Although Granddad had said the day would come when Blue Sky would leave them, Charlie did not want it to happen now. Granddad was not cured. Besides, he loved that little raven.

Charlie and Singing Bird searched for Blue Sky in the cottonwoods and pines until it was too dark to see. He was not to be found.

"Ooops," Singing Bird said, looking at her watch. "Late again." She ran through the willows and across the open sagebrush toward her home. Charlie sat down on Grand-dad's porch steps and dropped his arms on his knees and his head on his arms. Squeezing his eyes tightly shut he tried to gird himself against the pain of letting nature take its in-evitable course.

"I cannot stop Blue Sky," he repeated over and over. "I cannot stop him from doing what he has to do." Then he added, "And there will be no cure for Granddad."

Slowly he got to his feet, threw back his shoulders, and

walked to his cabin. He pushed back the half-open door and stood stock still. There on the foot of his bed sat Blue Sky and Pinecone. They were full of good food and sleeping.

Charlie grinned all the way to supper. Granddad would get well after all.

CHAPTER ELEVEN

Raven Power

The next day, softly edged snow clouds drifted down the mountains toward the valley. The lively little chipmunks disappeared down tunnels under Charlie's cabin. The porcupine climbed the cottonwood, and the last resident of the Day Care Center did not return to Granddad's trees to roost.

A message had been sent by the revolving earth. Snow is coming. Out on the sage flats the antelopes heard it. They gathered in large herds, preparing to leave the valley. On Bison Butte the bears heard it and sat down near their winter dens. The elk heard it. They moved into the trees.

Pinecone heard it. She did not come back to her juvenile home at the Day Care Center. The message told her to wander. She soared over the lodgepole pine forests at the foot of the Tetons. She flew east and looked over the resources on Goat Mountain. She circled above Granddad's ranch, hesitated, and flew on. She came to rest in a cottonwood tree along the Snake River. She huddled against the bole of the tree and fluffed her feathers. Snow began to fall.

Blue Sky did not get the message from the earth. He had a human mother who, unlike raven mothers, did not drive him off the territory. He spent the night on the footboard of Charlie's cot.

In the morning the world was white and Blue Sky did not leave for the day, as was his custom now. Instead he flew to Charlie's shoulder to say he wanted to go to breakfast. As they walked across the yard, he spoke in bird postures. He lifted his head feathers, spread his throat shackles, thumped his shoulders, and made himself look as impressive as a Sioux chieftain in a feathered warbonnet.

"Okay, boss bird," Charlie said. "That's nice of you to talk to me, but what's really important is that you want to eat with us again. Granddad needs you, he hasn't been feeling so well lately. He's always better when you're around."

Blue Sky gave two "knocks," to say "I'm me. I'm me."

"I know," said Charlie. "You are the center of the universe." He stroked his breast. "gro, gro, gro," said the raven.

"Good, let's eat." Charlie glanced into the cottonwood, hoping to see Pinecone, although he was certain he would not. When a young raven leaves home, Granddad had said, it is g-o-n-e.

"Snow," he sang out as he came into the ranch house. "Snow, Grandma Sally!"

"And you go home the day after tomorrow," she said. "I don't like that. I'll miss you."

"Your dad's coming for you Saturday," Granddad reminded him. Charlie nodded, and Blue Sky flew to Granddad's knee as he sat in the chair by the window.

"Welcome, fellow," Granddad said to the raven. Charlie sat down on the stool beside him.

"What'll happen to Blue Sky when I go?" he asked.

"He'll take care of himself," Granddad answered, "or he won't. That's how all life is."

Charlie blinked. "That's how all life is" did not seem good enough for his beloved bird.

"I don't want to go to school," he said. "I want to stay here all winter. Can I?"

"You're a scientist now. Go to school and see what happens."

"I want him to live," Charlie said and looked at Grandma Sally, hoping she would volunteer to take care of him. Granddad read his thoughts.

"She must not feed him," he said. "This is the absolute right time for him to leave and learn to survive. Right now, when all the other young ravens are learning."

"What about our study?" Charlie asked. He had never dared to tell him the Teton Sioux legend about ravens curing people. He knew his granddad would scoff. "I don't have the answer to whether ravens are good or bad."

"But you do," Granddad said.

"I do?"

"The answer is in your notes. Tally the good and bad deeds and tell me what you have."

"You mean I've studied the ravens long enough to know?"

"I won't say that."

"Good, because Singing Bird suggested another column—Mysterious. There are more checks in that column than the others."

"That's right," answered Granddad. "When you study, answers lead to mysteries, then answers and more mysteries."

Blue Sky flared his shoulders out and lifted his head like a president giving his State of the Union address.

"You're handsome," said Granddad, starting the chitchat.

While the ritual went on, Charlie went to the kitchen to get a cup of hot chocolate. Outside the window the pine siskins had gathered by the dozens at the bird feeder.

Grandma Sally saw him looking at them.

"They do that just before they leave for the winter," she said, and sighed.

After breakfast Blue Sky walked to the door, and Charlie opened it. He watched him fly west, thought about packing, then sat with Granddad and read the newspaper to him. He felt going-away sad and wondered if the migrating birds did too.

The next morning, although the snow had melted, it had changed the natural world around the ranch house. All was still. The ground squirrels were in their burrows, sliding into the deep sleep of hibernation. The pine siskins were gone, and Blue Sky was quiet, as if contemplating the earth's mood. He "grrrrred" softly in Charlie's ear as he rode on his shoulder to breakfast.

"Be sure to eat at Granddad's every day when I'm gone," Charlie said to him. "That way you'll both survive." He walked in the door, and Blue Sky flew to Granddad's knee.

He flashed his "head bonnet feathers" and let down the

long and shiny shackles on his legs and throat. He bowed and touched his head to Granddad's head.

"Thank you," Granddad said. "I greet you too." Then Blue Sky opened his beak. "knock, knock, knock"—"Look at me. Look at me."

"Blue Sky," Granddad said in astonishment. "The inside of your mouth is almost black." He turned to Charlie. "Know what that means?"

"That Blue Sky's a boss bird," Charlie said. "But isn't he too young? I thought a raven had to be an adult to have a black mouth."

"Not when he's got someone to boss. And the blacker the mouth the bossier the bird."

"Who's he bossing?" asked Charlie. "There are no other ravens around. Not even Pinecone. She's left us."

"Me," said Granddad and grinned. "He bosses me. I'm just realizing that."

"I've known that for a long time," said Grandma Sally.

"I thought you were his dad," Charlie said, "and I was his mom."

"I'm his peon," Granddad said. "And you're not his mom anymore. He's outgrown that stage. You're something else in the life of a raven. Something important, but I don't know what it is. List it under Mysterious."

"Put it under a new column—Unpredictable," said Grandma Sally. "I just can't keep up with all that raven's doings. He does this, he does that, he goes here, he goes there—he keeps changing."

"Unpredictable is the real truth, Grandma Sally," Charlie said. "I'm going to write that down. Ravens are totally and completely unpredictable."

Blue Sky flashed his ears again and flew to the back of Granddad's big chair, where he was higher than Granddad. He knocked importantly.

"Yes, sir, boss," Granddad said, his eyes bright with the wonder of raven behavior. "What can I do for you?"

Blue Sky flew to his chair at the dining table then onto the plate that Grandma Sally had filled with his food. Granddad joined him. Blue Sky ate so ravenously that Charlie asked if a storm could be coming. He had never seen Blue Sky eat so much so fast.

"I would say, yes," mused Granddad. "Wild animals have inner barometers. They can sense a storm before it gets here. And when they feel the big one coming that will lock up the valley until spring, they are ready for it. The grizzlies are in their beds, the elk are in the valleys, and the beavers are eating aspen bark in their lodges. Animals sense things we can't," he said and shook his head in admiration.

"Write it down," said Blue Sky.

Then the pills came out and Blue Sky grabbed the orange one, Grandma Sally squeezed juice, Granddad swallowed juice and pills. That over, Blue Sky flew down to the kitchen floor and walked to the door. Charlie opened it and he flew away.

The next morning the mountains and valley were covered with snow. Charlie, with Blue Sky riding on his head, walked slowly to breakfast, wishing the snow had buried the school. Tomorrow was Saturday. He had to go back to Jackson and leave Blue Sky.

"Hi, Grandma Sally," he said as he entered the kitchen and Blue Sky flew to Granddad. "Good news. It snowed four inches last night."

"The shovels are ready," she said. "I brought them inside last night."

Charlie and Grandma Sally waited at the table for Granddad and Blue Sky to complete their morning ritual. The greeting and chitchat over, Blue Sky flew to his chair ahead of Granddad. He was boss. He flicked his wings, lifted his feathers, and gobbled everything Grandma Sally had put out for him by the time Granddad sat down.

Then the pill plate came. Blue Sky "grrrrred" and "gurgled." Granddad chuckled, and the pill routine began. Grandma Sally went to the kitchen counter and squeezed oranges. Granddad pushed the pill plate away and grumbled. The grumble was Blue Sky's cue. He grabbed the orange pill and held it in his beak. Granddad reached to take it, but he wasn't fast enough. Grandma Sally returned with the juice, and Blue Sky was on the floor. Charlie opened the door and he was gone.

"I'm glad to see Granddad and Blue Sky playing the pill game again," said Grandma Sally.

"So am I," said Charlie. "Granddad is actually better when he plays it."

"That's what I've been thinking too," she said. "I'm beginning to think ravens really can cure."

A rhythmical rap sounded on the door.

"Come in, Singing Bird," Charlie called. She took off her boots and sat down at the table.

"I'm here for two reasons," she said. "One to say goodbye to Charlie."

"ca,ca,ca,ca,ca," Charlie answered, and frowned.

"Kmmmm gurgle," said Singing Bird, and her black lashes shaded the sparkle in her eyes.

"And the other," she went on, "is to tell everyone they're invited to a teepee ceremony on October eighteenth. That's the night before Dad takes down the teepee and we go to South Dakota." She picked up a biscuit and looked at Charlie. "Mom has already invited your folks—and guess what?—Andy wants to come. I didn't think he would. I thought he wanted to snowboard every night."

"Not at night anymore," said Charlie. "Not since he broke his arm last year snowboarding the Jackson ski slope under floodlights."

"Is it really snowboarding season again?" Grandma Sally asked. "Time goes so fast." She reached for Granddad's hand.

CHAPTER TWELVE

The Raven Owners' Drum

Charlie's dad drove a reluctant son back to Jackson Saturday morning, but by Monday Charlie was glad to be with his friends and back in school.

Through September he watched the early snowstorms fall and melt but hold fast on the mountain peaks. With each storm the snow line moved lower until by mid-October the great range was alabaster white. The valley, however, was snowless.

Charlie returned to the ranch every weekend. Mysteriously Blue Sky appeared when he arrived and disappeared when he left. Where did he go? Grandma Sally said she never saw him all week, and she never saw Pinecone at all.

On the night of October 17, the storm arrived that would lock up the valley until spring. The snow poured out of the sky like a waterfall from dusk until dawn. It stopped just after sunup and started again an hour later. This time it rode horizontally on raging winds. That morning, the day of the Teepee Festival, Charlie arrived from town on the snowplow. He jumped down into deep powder and waved good-bye to Jerry, the driver. Tramping toward the house, he pounded a path to the door. He sent the snow sparkling up from his boots to fall back down with the snow from the clouds.

"quork, quork, quork." Blue Sky flew over his head and, ignoring the snow, alit on the roof.

"Blue Sky!" Charlie stopped packing the trail. "Well, I shouldn't be surprised. It's the weekend, and so here you are!"

Blue Sky clucked, "quork, quork, quork"—"It's me. I'm here." Charlie held up his hand, and his now radiantly beautiful friend dropped gently onto it. They exchanged loving raven "kmmmms" all the way to Granddad's porch steps. Then Blue Sky flew to the roof.

"Come on in," Charlie said to him. "Granddad needs you." Blue Sky did not even glance at Charlie. He hopped

and flapped to the ridge, toppled onto his back, and slid down the snowy incline. He caught himself at the end, flew back, and slid down again.

"Grandma Sally! Granddad!" Charlie shouted as he ran into the house, greeted them hastily, and beckoned. "Come outside," he said. "Come see what Blue Sky's doing." Grandma Sally threw on her down parka and ran out into the blizzard.

"Write it down!" Blue Sky yelled, took off from the roof, and flew to the big cottonwood tree.

"Write what down?" Grandma grumped at Blue Sky. "That you can fly to a tree? What's so great about that?"

"Gosh," Charlie commented. "He was sledding—getting on his back and sledding—down the roof. Now look at him—just sitting. Who was it that said ravens are unpredictable?" He glanced at Grandma Sally. "That's the best observation ever made."

Blue Sky took two backflips off the limb, slid into a half roll, and landed on the roof of Charlie's cabin.

"And that proves I'm right," she said. "Blue Sky just performed like an acrobat, not a bird. Unpredictable!" She shook her head and gathered an armload of wood. "Where're your folks, Charlie?"

"They'll be here as soon as Dad gets them plowed out," he said and picked up the snow shovel to clear the porch. "They sent me ahead to help you."

"Put down the shovel. That can wait," Grandma Sally said. "The sourdough pancakes, ham, eggs, cheese, and orange juice cannot." Blue Sky slid down the roof on his back again, snow flew up from his wings, he took a swan dive off the eaves, and landed on Charlie's shoulder.

"Amazing!" Grandma Sally said, then pleadingly, "Blue Sky, please come to breakfast. Granddad's not been feeling well. You haven't been back to see him. And he's so much better when you visit." She picked up the broom, a permanent winter fixture by the door, and brushed snow off her boots before going into the house.

Granddad was dozing in his chair by the window. Blue Sky flew from Charlie's shoulder to his knee. Granddad awoke with a start and, smiling broadly, touched his head to Blue Sky's head.

"Hello, beautiful bird, where have you been? I don't see you all week. Are you like Charlie and only visit on weekends?" Up went Blue Sky's black glistening head bonnet.

"I miss you." Down went the throat and leg feathers. "I think you're great." Blue Sky gave several undulating "quorks" meaning, "I am here. Take notice."

"You look splendid," Granddad continued in a singsong voice. "Your feathers shine like jewels and your eyes are bright and clear. You look presidential."

"Write it down," said Blue Sky and flew to his place at the table. Granddad took his chair, making sure he sat with his head lower than Blue Sky's. He knew his station in this raven's world.

Blue Sky ate daintily, taking small pieces of food in his beak and swallowing them quietly.

"Hey, look how nicely he's eating," Charlie observed. "That's new. What's he up to?"

"Something unpredictable," said Grandma Sally. "Beware the raven. Isn't that what Mr. Spinder said?" She chuckled and gave Blue Sky a piece of pancake dripping with butter.

The pill dish came out. Blue Sky grabbed the orange pill, Granddad reached to take it from him, then Grandma Sally squeezed juice and handed it to him. Down went the pills. Blue Sky flew to the floor and walked to the door with Charlie, who let him out. But this time Charlie followed him. He was beginning to suspect Blue Sky of chicanery.

Suddenly a cloud of snow blew into Charlie's face. When he had wiped it away, Blue Sky was nowhere to be seen. "Morphed into sky," he said and scratched his head.

Charlie went inside and threw his bag on the cot in Grandma Sally's sewing room, where he slept in winter. His little cabin had no stove, and winter temperatures could drop to thirty and forty below zero. Although there were three bigger bedrooms for his parents, Andy, and visitors, Charlie chose this room because it looked out on the mountains.

When the snow stopped falling, Charlie fought back the winter. He shoveled snow off porch and steps, stacked firewood in the bin by the stove, and shook snow from the aspen and pine limbs to keep them from breaking. He did not dig a path from the house to the cars but packed the snow with his feet. Packed snow was the best footing.

While he worked he watched for Blue Sky. Once he saw

a single raven being chased by a pair of ravens. The pair called the three short rapid "quorks" that meant "Get out of here, get out of here. My territory." The single raven left. The pair danced and tumbled above the white landscape then dove into the pines on Bison Butte.

"Blue Sky's parents," he said and wondered if the single raven was Blue Sky or even Pinecone. No one had seen Pinecone for a long time, but since he could not see bands on the single raven he knew he could only guess. But, of course, he did not dare write that down.

Charlie's parents and Andy arrived in time for lunch. His brother, who had the brown eyes and strong wiry body of his mom, was out of the blue truck and into the snow in one antelope leap.

"Where's Blue Sky?" he called to Charlie.

"He's around here somewhere," Charlie said. "Help me find him." He led his brother in a wide circle around Granddad's house, peering into pine trees and under eaves.

"Maybe he left," Charlie said. "I think I saw his parents chase him away."

"His mom and dad chased him away?" Andy put his mittened hands on his hips. "That's mean."

"It's Good," said Charlie. "It's time for him to leave home and seek his fortune. All kids have to do that."

On the south side of the house where the wind had blown the ground clear of snow, a solitary golden dandelion stood. Charlie picked it. "I'm going to take this to Granddad," he told Andy. "He admires these hardy survivors."

Grandma Sally whistled her shrill call from the porch.

"Good," said Andy. "Lunch is ready. I'm starving."

Chris had come out to fetch wood for the stove. He walked back inside with Charlie.

"I've been meaning to tell you how proud of you I am," he said. "You made your granddad one happy man this summer. He feels like a naturalist again what with Blue Sky to study and you to talk to him and learn."

"I love him," said Charlie. "I just want to make him well."

That evening as the sun was setting behind the mountains the rhythmical beat of native drums sounded across the sagebrush.

"Let's go," Charlie said as he dried and put away the pan he had scrubbed clean. "We're being summoned."

Andy passed his mom at the door. "I'm walking," he said. "The road's plowed." Out he went.

Charlie put a log on the woodstove and banked the fire for the night. A wave of excitement ran down his spine. Every year at this time Flying Cloud held a ceremonial evening honoring the earth, the sky, and the animal spirits. Charlie loved this night. After it was over he always saw the world differently, and right now, he needed some insight. He had read over his notes during the week, and the categories Good and Bad and even Mysterious were not making sense. One was eclipsing the other. Ravens were ravens, his notes seemed to say.

Grandma Sally pulled the truck up to the porch and Charlie and Chris helped Granddad into it. He had to be

driven although the teepee was not far. As Charlie closed
the door on Granddad's side, he heard the feather rustle
that said "You're disturbing me." The sound came from under the porch eaves. Charlie leaped onto the porch.

"Blue Sky!" he said, peering into the dark. "So this is
where you go when no one can find you?"

The bird shook his feathers again.

"Okay, okay, I'm bothering you." He jumped off the
porch and climbed into the truck. His eyes were bright as a
crystal ball. He knew where Blue Sky slept.

Grandma Sally drove onto the plowed road and stopped.
Not far away stood the teepee. It glowed yellow-orange
like a Japanese paper lantern on the snow.

"Beautiful," she said, then drove slowly up to the round
teepee door.

After Granddad was helped from the truck he insisted on waiting until everyone but he and Charlie were in the teepee, then he walked to his seat on his own. Charlie followed, ready to help if necessary and hoping that Granddad's spurt of energy was because Blue Sky was back. Write it down, he said to himself.

The small fire in the teepee threw a low light, so it took several minutes for Charlie's eyes to adjust. Flying Cloud was seated by the altar with a buffalo skin robe across his shoulders. He wore a beaded loincloth and elegant ankle bracelets of fur and silver. His headpiece was a fan of eagle feathers in a narrow line from forehead to the nape of his neck. Across from him stood Soaring Swallow in her white deerskin dress. Fringes hung from the sleeves. The silver belt she wore was so long it rounded her waist and fell to her ankles. Her boots were elaborately decorated with dyed porcupine quills. Tonight her hair lay in one braid down her back. A cape of turquoise beads lay on her chest. She knelt beside Singing Bird, who also wore her beautiful white deerskin dress.

Charlie greeted his hosts with a raised hand, then he sat down cross-legged on the men's side of the teepee. Beside him was his dad, then Andy, and beyond him—Mr. Spinder! Charlie gawked and looked across the room. Mrs. Spinder sat with Grandma Sally and his mom.

"Boy, write THAT down," he mumbled. "The raven haters are sitting with the raven lovers." He glanced at Singing Bird for an explanation. She was looking at her father.

Flying Cloud arose. He chanted in a deep melodious

voice and turned to the four cardinal points of the earth: north, south, east, and west. His chants told of their significance, and Charlie felt he was being bonded with the earth and everyone present—even Mr. Spinder. He wondered if that was the reason Mr. and Mrs. Spinder had been invited to this ceremony of oneness.

Flying Cloud then stood before Granddad and, holding his hands to the heavens, sang these words in English.

> *"In the house of long life, there I wander.*
> *In the house of happiness, there I wander.*
> *Beauty before me, with it I wander,*
> *Beauty behind me, with it I wander.*
> *Beauty below me, with it I wander.*
> *Beauty above me, with it I wander.*
> *Beauty all around me, with it I wander.*
> *In old age traveling, with it I wander.*
> *On the beautiful trail I am, with it I wander."*

When the song was over Flying Cloud stood quietly for a long moment.

"That is a Navajo song," he said. "It's part of the Twelfth Dance in the Mountain Chant. When all the dances are carried out properly that song has the power to transform a sick person into a healthy one. I talked on the phone to the Navajo chief yesterday. He said the Navajos on the reservation had completed the dance properly this month. I have completed the song." He looked up at the sky through the smoke hole. He did not look at Granddad.

But Charlie felt hope. Granddad would get well. He glanced at Singing Bird, waiting for her to tell the story of the sick woman who was cured by the raven. That would let the Spinders know the value of ravens. But Singing Bird just sat on her heels and smiled.

Soaring Swallow picked up two globular rattles decorated with fur and feathers and gave them to Flying Cloud. Then she took the small black drum from the box that held the Raven Owners' artifacts, and Singing Bird threw some cedar twigs on the fire. The teepee filled with the clean odor of the plains.

Flying Cloud spoke.

"The dance I am about to perform was taught to me by a Raven Owner. It is a dance telling of the connection between raven and mankind." Now Charlie knew why the Spinders were asked.

Flying Cloud bent his knees into a deep crouch and, low to the ground, danced vigorously. The rattles "whooshed" like raven wings. Finally he jumped to his feet, and holding one arm high, slowly clicked his tongue to make the "knock, knock, knock" of the raven call. Then he bowed and opened his arms.

"I don't get it," said Mr. Spinder.

A sudden northeast wind blew smoke down the smoke hole. Everyone's eyes burned. Mr. Spinder coughed. Singing Bird arose and stepped outside. With a flip of the two long poles attached to the smoke flaps, she faced them to the southwest and the smoke poured out. The air in the teepee cleared.

Singing Bird took the Raven Owners' drum from her mother and returned it to its box. She faced the guests.

"I am going to tell you a story," she said.

"In a valley long ago the animals were dying of starvation. They did not know how to change their terrible destiny.

"One day Raven came into the valley with a mouthful of corn. He had eaten his fill and so he dug a hole and cached the leftovers for another day. But he didn't come back to get them, and when spring came the corn grew tall and flourished. Hare ate its leaves. Deer ate its tassels. Antelope ate its kernels.

"When Raven came back to the valley years later, coyote, wolf, bear, and wolverine cried out, 'Do something for us too. We meat eaters are starving.'

"'Follow me,' Raven said, and led them to a fallen bison that had thrived on the corn. With their strong teeth, they tore open the carcass, and not only did they eat, but Raven did too. Then they all napped—all except Raven. He carried off the last small bits of the feast and hid them in holes and under rocks and plants. Insects found the hidden food and multiplied. Reptiles found the insects and multiplied. Birds found the insects, the corn, and even the meat, and multiplied.

"And all because Raven came to the valley."

Singing Bird bowed to the four corners of the earth and sat down on her heels.

Charlie smiled. He knew that story was meant for one person—Mr. Spinder.

"I get it," Mr. Spinder said. "That's a good lesson. We should all store things for a rainy day."

"It sounded like an ecology lesson to me," said Granddad.

"The lesson is—ravens are good," said Grandma Sally.

Charlie didn't speak. He was pondering whether ravens were Good or Bad—or neither.

Flying Cloud now prepared his pipe of peace to pass around the circle. Charlie wondered if he was going to let Mr. Spinder smoke it. Only friends shared the sacred pipe. He waited to see.

The pipe was long and white. Along its carved stem, tassels hung on strings of beads. They danced when Flying Cloud tamped the tobacco in the bowl. That done, he leaned gracefully over the fire, lit a pine stick, and then the pipe. He took a long draft of smoke and slowly blew it out. He passed the sacred pipe to his left. Granddad put it to his lips and took two long draughts. Then he passed the pipe to his left. Mr. Spinder took a draught. So he is a friend, Charlie thought. Perhaps Flying Cloud knew that this raven-friendly environment would affect Mr. Spinder. That's what Granddad thought Charlie's study would be about.

Mr. Spinder passed the pipe to him by reaching over Andy's head.

"Don't smoke, Charlie," Granddad said. "You're too young. I took two smokes—one for you." He winked at Grandma Sally, as if it were something she had planned.

"You took a smoke for Andy," Charlie said, and pulled on the pipe, coughed, and started it back through the men to the women. They passed it on to their left as they too smoked the sacred pipe of peace. And as it moved, there was a feeling of peace in the teepee. Even Mr. Spinder's face showed goodwill.

Charlie thought about the ritual of passing the pipe always to the left. Routine, he said to himself. Both ravens and humans live by routine. Good? Bad? Mysterious? Or just plain the best way to live?

Flying Cloud sprinkled blue cornmeal on the altar, and the ceremony was over.

Mr. Spinder then turned to Granddad and shook his hand.

"By the way," he said. "My name is Alfred, Alfred Spinder. Call me Al, and my wife would like to be called Liza. May I call you Will?"

"Makes sense," said Granddad. Al helped him up and through the low round door. Outside in the night the snow crystals reflected back the light of an eternity of stars. The effect was so bright that Granddad could see the bumper sticker on the Kentons' truck. It read: STANDING ROCK MIDDLE SCHOOL GIRLS' AND BOYS' BASEBALL TEAM.

"Good team," he said.

Charlie's dad was pulled out of the teepee by Andy, who was eager to get home.

"What's the big hurry?" Granddad asked his grandson.

"Snowboard race tomorrow," Andy said, and held up his thumbs.

"And believe it or not, he wants to get his sleep," said Chris.

Nancy came out of the teepee, kissed Granddad and Grandma good night and climbed into the red truck with Chris and Andy. They knew Charlie would be staying at Granddad's. When they had driven off, Mr. Spinder turned to Granddad.

"You're a naturalist, I hear," he said. "My brother and I bought a commercial tree farm. Maybe someday you or your son could look at it and give us some advice."

"Where is it?"

"South of here on the other side of the mountain range. My brother lives in Idaho and thought this was a good buy."

"What kind of trees?"

"Red fir. Good money in red fir."

Granddad looked up at the endless spangle of stars, wondering if he should worry this man, then thought he should.

"There's been an outbreak of army cutworms in that area. I hope you didn't buy a pig in a poke."

"No, I sure didn't. My brother and I had a forester check out everything. Good healthy trees. Also beautiful. Liza and I are going to spend the winter in the house there. It's very up-to-date."

"Warmer?"

"Well, that, and also it has a laundry, dishwasher, and a video and computer room." He looked back at the teepee. "I wonder what's delaying Liza. It's cold."

In the warm teepee Liza was chatting amiably with Grandma Sally and Soaring Swallow. Charlie interrupted to tell his grandmother that he would walk home later. Flying Cloud had asked him to stay and help put out the fire and lace up the teepee.

"That's fine," she said, and Singing Bird escorted the two women outside and returned to the fire. The four were now alone.

"Sit down, Charlie. Sit down, Singing Bird," Flying Cloud said and sat himself cross-legged on the south side of the glowing embers.

"Singing Bird has a story to tell you, Charlie," he said and opened the box that held the Raven Owners' drum and lance. She sat down and folded her hands in her lap.

"Long, long ago," she began, looking up at the stars shining through the smoke hole, "a young Lakota Sioux chieftain met the first Raven.

" 'If you take me into your tribe and share food with my kind,' Raven said, 'I will warn you of enemies.'

"His enemies, the Ojibwe tribes, lived on the Great Plains where the chieftain lived. The Ojibwes had won many battles and killed many of the chieftain's warriors. The chieftain liked Raven's offer and adopted him into his tribe.

"One day when Raven was flying over the land, he saw an army of Ojibwes in warbonnets. They were sneaking through a hilly pass. He flew to Chieftain and yelled the raven cry that meant 'enemy.'

" 'Show me where,' said the chieftain. Raven soared, then

pointed one wing toward the hills and held the other wing close to his body. The chieftain led his warriors where Raven had wing-tipped and took the enemy from behind. His victory was great. The Ojibwes never returned. Chieftan named his tribe—Raven Owners.

"Ever after, boys who wanted to join the tribe were tested for their knowledge of ravens before they could become a Raven Owner. Those who passed were given a small black drum."

Singing Bird stood up.

"Stand up, Charlie," Flying Cloud said.

By the faint orange light of the embers, Charlie saw Flying Cloud take the rare and precious black drum out of its box and walk up to him.

"You are now a Raven Owner," he said and gave him the drum.

Charlie blinked back tears until he could speak. Then he looked up at Flying Cloud.

"I have a very short story to tell you."

"What is it?"

"This is the honor of my life."

CHAPTER THIRTEEN

The Raven Cache

Early the next morning Charlie took the Raven Owners' drum out of his pack and turned it over and over in his hands. He could not believe it was his. When he thought about its meaning, he felt guilty. He did not know enough about ravens to have earned it.

"But I will," he said.

When he was dressed he carried the drum outside and tapped its surface. *Whoosh, whoosh, whoosh,* it sounded.

"Wow," he said. "That sounds like raven wings. Cool."

Feathers rustled and Blue Sky flew out from his hideout under the eaves and lit on the woodpile. He cocked an eye at the drum.

"Know what this drum means to me?" Charlie said to him. "It means I am really going to earn it. I am really going to learn all about ravens, and you're going to help me." Blue Sky preened a wing feather.

"Today," Charlie went on, "you, Granddad, and I are running an experiment. I want to know for sure if you get upset when I change your routine." Blue Sky ran his beak down another ebony feather. It snapped back in place like a folding Japanese fan, and he flew to Charlie's head. He rode there to the ranch house and down the hallway to the sewing room. There Charlie carefully put the drum far back on a shelf where it would be safe.

Granddad was in his chair when Charlie and Blue Sky came into the living room. After listening to the proposed experiment Granddad eagerly agreed to it, so Charlie asked Granddad to stand up.

"I want to see what happens," Charlie said, "when you greet Blue Sky on your feet instead of seated." Granddad chuckled and stood right up. Blue Sky, seeing no knee to sit on, flew to the back of a chair and lifted his "ears." He was miffed.

Granddad went on with his usual routine.

"You look very handsome," he said. Blue Sky turned his back on him.

"Your feathers are shiny and long," Granddad went on. Blue Sky drooped his wings.

"Your beak shines like polished ebony." Blue Sky lifted his bonnet. "ca,ca,ca,ca,ca."

"Whoops," said Charlie. "He is mad, really mad. That's his worst cuss word."

"Your mouth is getting darker, boss man," Granddad cooed on, "and you are bossier than ever." Blue Sky flew to Granddad's desk and tore up a letter before Charlie could stop him.

"That's enough proof," Charlie said. "Thanks, Grand-dad. Blue Sky's a perfectionist. He likes things just so."

"He wants things his way, not ours," said Granddad. Having said that he sat down smiling and shaking his head, and Blue Sky flew right to his knee.

"Gorgeous, handsome raven," said Granddad, and emotions being short-lived in birds, Blue Sky flared out his throat and pantaloon feathers in praise of himself. Charlie gave the torn letter to Grandma Sally to be taped together.

The breakfast table routine went along according to Blue Sky's agenda—the food, the pill dish, Granddad grumbling, the orange pill snatched and Granddad resnatching it, then the pills washed down with juice.

Or was this what was really going on? Charlie wondered. He had an eerie feeling that he was not seeing everything. What's with the pills? he asked himself. With Singing Bird's story still fresh in his mind about raven's caching their food, he followed Blue Sky to the door and let him out. Charlie went back inside and watched him through the window.

Blue Sky hopped down the steps, flew to a pile of snow, walked down it, looked around, and walked back up. He poked a hole in the snow, changed his mind, and flew to the woodpile. A noise from inside the ranch house alarmed him, and he winged to Charlie's cabin and lit on the steps. He cocked his eye and after a seemingly thoughtful pause, flew to the snowless top ledge of the window. There he tamped something a few times and departed.

"Ah-ha!" Charlie was out the door, across the snow, and

into the toolshed in a minute. He got a ladder, put it against his cabin, climbed it, and found an orange pill lying on the top of the window trim.

Now he was excited. He was almost sure he knew what was happening, but he didn't dare take a guess. Instead he went to his room, took out his notebooks, and made two columns on a blank piece of paper.

The days Granddad felt good he labeled one, and *The days Granddad felt poorly* he wrote above the other. Then he paged through his notes and put down the dates when Blue Sky had had breakfast with Granddad and how Granddad had felt afterward. Next he recorded the days Blue Sky did not breakfast with Granddad and how Granddad felt that day.

"Wow," he said when all the data was before him. "It's absolutely true. Granddad feels good when Blue Sky comes to breakfast with him. He feels bad when he doesn't.

Why?" And he grinned a broad grin. "Because Blue Sky's been stealing his orange pills.

"Singing Bird is right, ravens cure!

"And now to find out why the orange pills make Granddad feel worse." He closed his notebooks, tucked them in his backpack, and sought out Grandma Sally, who was baking cookies in the kitchen.

"Grandma Sally," he said. "I was looking at my notes. When Blue Sky comes to breakfast, Granddad is better."

"Of course," she said. "He loves that bird. Pets make us feel better."

"Yes," Charlie said. "But have you ever heard anything about one medicine interacting with another to make a person sicker?"

"Yes, I've read about it, and the pharmacist warns about mixing drugs all the time. Why?"

"When Blue Sky ate with Granddad, do you remember where he went when he left the table?"

She pondered. "Sometimes he goes to the door, sometimes he goes to—" She walked to the counter and pulled back the cookie jar.

"Charlie!" Three orange pills were behind the jar. She moved the box that held matches. Two more. Another was behind her recipe box.

"Wooo, this makes me a bad housekeeper. I never noticed the pills. And I'll bet they're all over the house—and outside too.

"But how could he do this?" she asked. "Granddad always snatched back the orange pill and swallowed it."

"No, I didn't," shouted Granddad, who had been listening in his chair by the window. "I hate those pills. Always thought they made me sicker."

"But I saw you take them"—Grandma Sally paused—"I thought."

"Not those orange ones. You always had your back turned squeezing oranges when Blue Sky snatched them." Granddad chuckled. "Now call the doctor right away. Tell him that a raven ran an experiment on me that he should have done." He laughed at the crazy situation.

"Is this the conclusion to our question 'how the environment affects humans'?" Charlie asked.

Granddad chuckled. "I think you can answer that," he said, and took out his little black notebook, wrote in it, and then looked up.

"And, Charlie," he went on, "speaking of caching things, I tucked a piece of venison fillet in the freezer. It's under the trout. Give it to Blue Sky."

"Frozen?"

"Yes, frozen."

"But how can he eat frozen meat?"

"What do you think ravens do in winter? Stick it in the microwave?" Charlie grinned and went to get the meat.

"Granddad," he said, "you must think Blue Sky is 'Good' to hide your pills. Can I put that down in the Good column?"

"No," answered Granddad. "He is being a raven, caching things—and I, like the wolf, am rewarding him with fillet of venison."

"But he doesn't eat the orange pills like Singing Bird's raven ate the bison. So why does he steal and hide them?"

"They're pretty," Granddad said.

"Yeah," said Charlie, his eyes opening wide, "that's it." And he ran to his room for his notebooks. Turning the pages he found what he was looking for and came back to Granddad.

"'June twenty-seventh,'" he read aloud. "'Blue Sky carried one of Singing Bird's pretty earrings up on Granddad's roof and hid it. I went up to get it but couldn't find it.'"

"You wrote that down?"

"Yes."

"Good. Anything more?"

"Yes. I wrote this: 'July fourteenth. Blue Sky took Singing Bird's earring out of hiding and played with it.'"

"And when he was done did he hide it again?" asked Granddad.

"Yes."

"And you never saw where he put it."

"No. He would never hide anything when I was looking."

"You've solved that mystery," he said. "I feel better when Blue Sky comes to breakfast because he steals and hides my wretched orange pills. Good work."

"We still have mysteries," Charlie said. "Now we've got to find out where Blue Sky goes when I'm in town."

"Now you're on my study—where do young ravens go when they leave their parents. It would be nice if you solved it, but before you tackle that mystery, you need to find out who you are in Blue Sky's timeless raven world."

"I'm his mom."

"Not anymore. He's graduated from kindergarten. You are something more essential—something that's connected to the ancient past of ravens, whatever it may be."

"Granddad, you sound like Mr. Spinder."

"Al," he said and winked.

Charlie sighed. The Raven Owners' drum was difficult to earn.

CHAPTER FOURTEEN

The Ancient Connection

By late December the snow was four feet deep in Teton Valley and still piling up. It was Friday afternoon. Charlie was in history class, doodling in his raven notebook and waiting for class to end so he could catch the snowplow to Granddad's and save his dad a trip. What's more, he liked to be with Jerry, the snowplow man. Jerry saw just about every species of Rocky Mountain wildlife as he plowed the wilderness roads, and he knew a lot about them.

Charlie drew an X for Granddad's ranch house and another X for his school. He wrote down the distance between the two, as the raven flies, fifteen miles, and in Singing Bird's Mysterious column he wrote:

December 17. Where is Blue Sky during the week? He turns up at Granddad's almost at the same instant I do— and yet he is not at Granddad's from Monday through Friday. Grandma Sally checked under the porch eaves during the week and he's not there. So where does he spend his weekdays?

This evening Jerry, our snowplow man, is going to take me the long way to Sagebrush Flats Road. He said he'd seen flocks of ravens over near Morton. They were feeding on carcasses of bison or elk. Maybe Blue Sky's among them.

I keep wondering just what role I play in Blue Sky's life now that Granddad says I'm no longer his mom. I have the eeriest feeling about it. Score one for the supernatural and Mr. Spinder.

The bell rang, and school was over for Christmas vacation. Parkas were thrown on, snowboards grabbed, packs shouldered, and in fifteen minutes the corridors were empty of kids. It was winter in the mountain valley.

In five minutes Charlie was on Jerry's snowplow.

"Your grandma wants you to pick up her groceries at Smiley's Grocery Store," Jerry said as he drove the snowplow truck slowly down the county road to the store. Charlie jumped out and returned in several minutes with two brown paper bags that he put on the floor at his feet. Jerry drove on in the fiery glow of a red sunset. As they passed the marshes on the outskirts of town, Charlie looked at the frozen home of the trumpeter swans. There were only a few hundred of these gorgeous white birds left on earth, and no one seemed to know how to bring them back. The pair had flown south with the first snow, but Charlie liked to close his eyes and pretend they were still there.

"Funny thing," Jerry said as he shifted gears to climb out of the lowlands. "A bunch of ravens landed on the store roof when you were in there. These seemed to be looking for something, poking and flipping snow and stuff. When I got out to clean the headlights they flew away."

"Ravens at the grocery store," said Charlie. "I wonder if Mr. Smiley feeds them on the roof like Grandma Sally does?"

"I don't think so," said Jerry. "He thinks ravens are pests."

"Hmmm," mumbled Charlie. "One more item in the Mysterious column."

Jerry drove onto Crystal River Road, which ran along the south side of Bison Butte. The road crossed the frozen bottomlands and went along the rocky ridges south of Morton. Mule deer grazed on the windswept slopes of the butte. Three bighorn sheep stood motionless on the skyline like public statues.

Charlie was gladdened by the sight of the handsome animals—and then a raven flew by, and something like love surged through him. His heartbeat quickened, and he felt as if he could fly.

When they plowed the lane of one of Jerry's customers, a fishing guide, he asked him if he had seen any ravens lately.

"Ravens?" the man said. "There are enough ravens up at the warm springs in Slide Canyon to blacken a football field.

"Those birds are some kind of magic," he went on. "They turn somersaults in the air, flatten out and fly side by side in ribbons and triangles and half moons."

"That's raven stuff, all right," Charlie said. Then Jerry drove the snowplow toward the springs.

As they approached, a black cloud arose from a field.

"Ravens," said Charlie. "Hundreds of them. Gee, I'll never find Blue Sky."

The black wing feathers reflected back the red light of the low sun as the ravens circled and looped against the sky. Charlie thought he was watching fireworks.

"How do you like that?" said Jerry of the performance. "I've never seen that before."

Charlie jumped from the cab and plowed through the snow to the ravens' gathering field. Even in the twilight he could see why they had come there. Elk guts were strewn over the area. This was not the hunting season. Some poachers had brought their animals here to butcher and had spread out the guts so the ravens and coyotes would clean up the evidence.

"Another score for the Good column," Charlie said to Jerry as he got back in the cab, then added, "if you're a poacher."

"What's this 'score for the Good column' all about?" Jerry asked.

"You know what?" Charlie said and laughed. "I really don't know. I've been doing a scientific study to find out if ravens are good or bad, but what I have found out so far is that ravens are ravens are ravens."

Jerry turned the snowplow around and drove north to Sagebrush Flats Road. Bison were huddled in dark clumps on the vast landscape of snow. They were digging with their sharp fore hooves and uncovering grasses. Ravens joined them, alighting in their diggings to pick up dormant insects.

The bison did not chase them off. As Charlie watched, Singing Bird's legend became real.

"Seems that the big mammals do like ravens," he said. "And ravens do like big mammals."

"Sure," said Jerry. "Animals give and take out here in the wilderness. They've worked something out over the ages, but as far as I'm concerned they are the only ones that know what it is."

"And I wish I knew and could tell you," Charlie said.

What I'd really like to know, he said to himself, is just who I am in Blue Sky's world. Then I would really have earned the Raven Owners' drum.

Jerry stopped the snowplow and reached for his binoculars. He focused them on a distant speck on the landscape, then handed them to Charlie.

"Mountain lion," he said. "Interesting. My snowplow buddies and I are seeing a lot of desperate winter activity. A mountain lion out in the flats by day is one of them."

" 'Desperate winter activity'?"

"The snow's so deep this year that the moose and deer can't find greens to eat. They're weak, and that brings on the predators. I've seen more wolves down from Yellowstone this winter than I've ever seen before—and now here's a mountain lion."

"He must be really hungry," said Charlie, "to be out in the daylight."

"I'm sure he is," Jerry said. "He's got a lot of competition."

It was almost dark when Jerry drove the snowplow up to Granddad's gate and Charlie jumped out.

"Come on in for dinner," he said. "Grandma invites you through me. There is always enough. She can make food appear endlessly."

"Thanks, but I've got to get back," he said. "Timber, my six-year-old, wants me to play with him tonight before he goes to bed."

The snowplow's headlights cut shafts in winter's early darkness as it departed through the walls of snow. A great horned owl called. Charlie took the tramped path to the ranch house porch.

Whoosh, whoosh, whoosh.

"Blue Sky!" The glistening black raven lit on his shoulder. "Where did you come from?" He looked back in the direction from which he had arrived and saw no answer to that question—no tree, no dwelling, only snow. "One more for the Mystery column," he said. "But I'm sure glad to see you. Let's eat."

With Blue Sky "grrrrrring" sounds of contentment in his ear, Charlie swept the snow off his boots and was reaching for the door when it opened. There stood Singing Bird.

"Hey," Charlie said, smiling broadly. "What are you doing here?"

"Dad and Mom wanted to come back to Sagebrush Flats for Christmas," she said.

Blue Sky brushed her face as he flew past her to Granddad.

"Blue Sky!" she exclaimed. "Oh, this is great. Blue Sky's still here."

He sailed right to Granddad's knee. Then he puffed his feathers and lifted his ears to show that he was of higher rank than Granddad.

"Yes, boss," he said and sat up straighter. Charlie gave Granddad a hug. "How are you feeling?"

"Not so good."

"But Blue Sky cured you, didn't he? Not quite the way I thought he would, but he did hide the orange pills and showed us that your mix of pills was wrong."

"He did, that young Hippocrates did do that," Granddad said, then added slowly, "but not even the magic of a raven can cure what I have."

Charlie dug his nails into his palms and in a low voice asked, "What is it?"

"An old heart slowing down." He looked out the big window.

> *"Beauty all around me, with it I wander.*
> *In old age traveling, with it I wander.*
> *On the beautiful trail I am, with it I wander."*

Charlie bit his lips tightly together. Grandma Sally saw him struggling with his feelings and stepped into the living room. She slipped an arm around his shoulder.

Granddad touched Blue Sky's beak.

"Let's talk," he said to the bird. "You look absolutely marvelous."

"grrrrrs" and "kmmmms," from Blue Sky. He flicked the nictitating membranes across his eyes as he made love gurgles; then he "quorked."

When Granddad ran out of words of praise, Grandma Sally put another plate on the table for Singing Bird, and they all sat down to dinner.

Monday came and Blue Sky did not leave.

"Seems to me," said Grandma Sally, "that when Charlie is here, Blue Sky is here."

"Ah," said Granddad. "That seems to be true, but let's test it. Charlie, why don't you go to town when Grandma goes shopping this afternoon and spend the night. We'll see if Blue Sky stays here."

"Go to town for a night when I can be out here?"

"I ran your experiment," Granddad said. "Now let's run mine."

"Well . . . ," Charlie said, procrastinating.

"You could help your mom get the Christmas tree and bring it out," said Grandma Sally, who was also eager to know what the results of the experiment would be.

Charlie spent that night in town.

The next morning the temperature had dropped so low the valley was sparkling with hoar snow. Tree limbs and buds, telephone poles and their wires, houses, cars, the empty Spinder ranch house glistened with feathery crystals.

Grandma Sally, as she had promised to do for her part in the experiment, stepped out the door before dawn to see if Blue Sky had spent the night under the eaves. He had not. She saw no raven, only the frosted world. She paused and gazed across the land.

As long as I live I will never get used to the beauty of winter up here in the mountains, she said to herself. Then she reported to Granddad that Blue Sky was not in his weekend roost.

"Progress," he said. "Now to observe what happens when Charlie comes back."

Seven hours later Charlie and Andy jumped out of their family's red truck and were untying the Christmas tree when Blue Sky flew down to its branches and landed on them as lightly as down. Nancy and Chris were looking to see where he had come from when Grandma Sally came out to greet them.

"Hey, Grandma," Charlie called. "Blue Sky spent the night, didn't he?"

"No."

"But he came down the minute I got out of the truck! He can't have been far away."

"Write it down!" shouted Blue Sky and flew to the ranch house roof. He gobbled a choice piece of cutthroat trout Grandma Sally had tossed there on the chance that he might spend the night and want a snack in the morning.

It was the day before Christmas Eve, and by Carlisle

family tradition too early to trim the tree. Charlie put it in its stand in the corner of the living room, pulled on his snow boots and gaiters, and went out to shovel snow and be with Blue Sky.

In the late afternoon the temperature dropped to ten below zero. Charlie stoked the woodstove until its radiant heat warmed the whole house. Blue Sky went to his porch roost early. The air crackled and the ice on the distant river boomed as it thickened. The porcupine left the far corner of the pump house and curled up under the warm pump, but not before chewing on one of Grandma Sally's wooden garden shoes.

Early on Christmas Eve Charlie went to the toolshed for the cedar Yule log he had cut last summer. As he approached the shed he saw the huge tracks of a mountain lion.

"Whoa," he said. "Lions don't come down here near people." Hoping to see the big cat he followed the tracks to the woodshed, around his cabin, and on to the bison fence. There they ended.

He can't be far, he said to himself and recalled Jerry's comment about "desperate winter activity." He shouldered the big log and carried it to the hearth. Granddad was cleaning the glass doors of the woodstove so the fire could be seen more clearly.

"Granddad," Charlie said. "There are mountain lion tracks going from the woodshed to the bison fence."

"Mountain lion." Granddad stopped wiping. "I haven't

seen one down here ever. That's bad—and I mean it. When cougars have to come this close to humans they're desperate—probably starving. Keep checking on him."

"Hallooo, halloo." Singing Bird and Soaring Swallow were knocking on the door.

"We're bringing our Prairie Gifts," Soaring Swallow said as she put three packages in the Festival Basket.

Together for Christmas, the Carlisles and the Kentons joined in a special festival. Each person, after months of thought and care, chose one of their dearest possessions to give on the holiday. The gifts were then wrapped and placed in Grandma Sally's Festival Basket. They bore no name, of neither the recipient nor the giver. On Christmas Day each person would choose one of the presents. After opening it, the giver would tell the story behind his gift. Sometimes the stories brought tears, sometimes laughter. No other presents were exchanged.

After Singing Bird and Soaring Swallow had put their presents in the basket and Nancy and Chris had gone off to their room to unpack, Andy helped Charlie string the tree lights.

Grandma Sally went outside to the toolshed for the folding table that traditionally held the Christmas venison and all the trimmings. She was struggling with the shed door when Blue Sky appeared, quorking and squawking. He sat on the woodpile—"REK,REK,REK." He then flew to the shed door. "REK,REK,REK,REK,REK." He kept up the noise until Grandma Sally became annoyed.

"Oh, stop!" she said, and bent over to look for the table. Blue Sky took to his wings, screaming louder and faster. Then, tipping his right wing at Grandma Sally, he croaked strange sounds and flew toward the woodshed.

"What's the matter with you?" Grandma shouted, and then it occurred to her that Blue Sky might be telling her something. She looked up. A mountain lion was crouched on the roof of the shed, his yellow eyes pinned on hers. He was poised to spring.

"Charlie!" she screamed, and backed away. Charlie, who

had heard the crazy cries of Blue Sky, was already on the porch. He heaved a piece of firewood at the lion.

The log hit the shed eaves, the mountain lion leaped into the snow and ran. Grandma Sally stood still. She wasn't shaking, but she was icy cold.

"Thank you, Blue Sky," she said and went in the house without brushing off her boots. She sat down on the stool beside Granddad. When she finished telling him how Blue Sky warned her that a mountain lion was about to attack, she was shivering.

Singing Bird picked up the telephone and called her dad. "String your bow and get an arrow," she said. "A mountain lion is headed your way."

Nancy brought Grandma Sally a glass of water, and Charlie put a hand on Granddad's trembling shoulder.

"That puts five marks in the Good column," Charlie said.

"Not so fast," cautioned Granddad. "Remember Singing Bird's legend? The raven led the wolf to the bison so he could eat too."

"You mean Blue Sky was telling the lion where Grandma was? Not telling Grandma where the lion was?"

"Leading predators to prey, and following predators to carcasses is ancient raven behavior."

Charlie was furious at Granddad for even thinking that. This was different. This was Blue Sky. Of course Blue Sky was warning Grandma. It had to be. He wanted it that way. Granddad was a scientist, but Charlie had lived with Blue Sky. He saw more than notes and data. He saw the beyondness of nature where the unimaginable happens. And he knew it had.

He looked at Grandma Sally and saw that she too thought Blue Sky had warned her.

"No, Granddad," he finally said with certainty, "Blue Sky knew what he was doing. He saved Grandma. I know that. I had just fed him. He wasn't even hungry." Granddad thought about that.

"That's mind-blowing," he said.

CHAPTER FIFTEEN

The Raven and the Boy

The tree was trimmed. The falling snow was decorating every window, and the venison roast was filling the cabin with mouth-watering smells. The scene was set for the traditional Carlisle/Kenton Christmas Festival, and the actors fit the scene. Singing Bird and Soaring Swallow were dressed in tan deerskin dresses trimmed with turquoise beads. Flying Cloud wore his chaps and leather shirt. Even Granddad had dressed up. He wore his eagle bola tie and a white shirt. Charlie, Andy, and Grandma Sally were in brand-new catalog clothes that still held the creases from being folded in a mail carton, and Blue Sky, on Granddad's knee, displayed his long shining throat feathers. Voices rose and the noise level grew so joyfully loud that Grandma Sally had to bang a wooden spoon on the cookie can to bring quiet.

"Dinner is served," she said.

Flying Cloud rose, walked to the big window, and lifted his arms. The snow swirled and danced outside. Throwing back his head he chanted a prayer praising the mysteries of life, one of which was Blue Sky saving Grandma from the mountain lion. He chanted in his native language, and only Singing Bird and Soaring Swallow understood how deeply he appreciated Raven's deeds. Then in English he said, "Time to eat."

After dinner and before dessert, presents were chosen. In respect for teepee tradition, they were opened to the left. This year Singing Bird began the opening. She had selected a small box. Carefully she removed the lid. In it lay an orange pill.

"It's from me," said Grandma Sally. "Finding that pill behind my recipe box is the best thing that ever happened to me. That's all. That's my story."

"Write it down," exclaimed Blue Sky, responding to the excitement in her voice.

"I'll write it down," said Granddad. "And I'll also write that the doctor agreed with a raven. A bad mix of pills." He raised a palm to Blue Sky and thanked him. Blue Sky lifted his shimmering black headdress and knocked three times. "I'm me. I'm me. I'm me. Behold." The inside of his mouth was noticeably darker. Granddad chuckled.

Singing Bird carefully replaced the orange pill in the box and blew Blue Sky a kiss. "Thank you, we all love Granddad."

Andy opened the biggest box and found another box inside another box inside another box. Finally he got to a season's ticket for the ski lift.

"That's my gift," Chris said, "and here's the story.

"I thought and thought until I suddenly thought of, not my favorite possession, but Andy's. He's been saving for a season's ski pass. So I'm putting a new twist on our Christmas this year—I'm giving somebody else's favorite present."

"But how did you know he would pick it?" Singing Bird asked.

"I put it in the biggest box I could find—and it worked."

Andy thumbed up, ran to his dad and hugged him. "Thanks."

Charlie was the last to open. He had selected his present early. He knew who had given it. Thrift was one of Granddad's strong points, and a small gift at the edge of the basket was wrapped in newspaper. Only Granddad would do that.

A perfectly round stone rolled out of the paper into his palm. Reddish in color and about an inch in diameter it had been worn round by natural forces. Charlie turned it over and over, smiling and tilting his head from side to side in total curiosity.

"It was made by nature, not man," said Granddad.

"I've never seen anything like it—a perfectly round stone from nature." He looked at Granddad for the story.

"When I was a boy," Granddad said, "my father, who was a geologist, took me on trips to rock outcrops and riverbeds, highway cuts and canyons.

"I grew bored with rocks. They didn't move. I knew my father didn't like me to feel that way so I tried to change. But I couldn't. The stones didn't lay eggs or have young. Then one day I came upon a round stone lying on a stream beach. I took it to Dad, hoping he would be pleased with my interest in stones.

" 'Look at this,' I said. 'It's perfectly round.' He held it up. 'Not perfectly round,' my father replied, and handed it back to me. I put it in my pocket and walked toward the stream.

"'Where are you going?' he called.

"'To find the perfect round stone,' I answered.

"'You'll never find it,' he said. 'Nature doesn't make perfect circles or perfect straight lines.'

"But I kept looking. The search took me into streams and I learned where the fish swam and the snails walked. The search took me to cliffs, and I learned where the swallows nested. The search took me up the mountains to alpine flowers. The search took me to the tailings at a badger den, and so, in searching for the perfect round stone, I became a naturalist."

Charlie leaned forward, waiting to hear the ending. Granddad leaned back in his chair to say he was done.

"So where did you find the perfect round stone?" Charlie asked.

"I didn't," Granddad answered.

"But—" Charlie held up the stone. "Here it is."

"Oh, yes," he said. "After years of searching, learning, and living, after loving, having children and grandchildren, I took that first stone out of the box—and it was perfect."

"Granddad, what are you saying?" Charlie asked in frustration.

"Think about it."

"Oh, gee." Charlie stood up and pulled Singing Bird to her feet.

"Let's eat dessert. I'll whip the cream," he said. "You cut the huckleberry pie."

At the end of the day, when Andy and his parents had returned to Jackson and the Kentons had snowshoed home to their ranch house, and when Blue Sky was under the porch roof, Charlie took out his notebook. He wrote:

December 25. I'm going to look for the perfect round stone! I mean the really, truly perfect round stone. And it has to do with ravens.

He was catching on to Granddad's maddening open-ended remark—"think about it."

The next morning before breakfast, Granddad tapped his barometer and studied the movement of the needle.

"A big storm is coming," he announced. "The atmospheric pressure is dropping fast."

Outdoors the biological barometers were already aware of the storm, although the sky was still bright and clear. Blue Sky knocked on the kitchen window to come in. Quill, the porcupine, rolled his feet and nose into his belly. With his quills thrust out to stab enemies, he went to sleep. The bison sought shelter under the trees along the irrigation ditch. The wolf curled up by a rock at the foot of Bison Butte and covered her bare nose with her tail. Under the snow near Charlie's cabin, four families of deer mice began tunneling toward one another. They met in Grandma Sally's snow-buried lettuce garden, and putting forefeet and hind legs around each other, tucking heads into bellies and under necks, twelve little mice made themselves into one big warm ball of body heat.

At noon purple-green clouds obscured the mountains. The blizzard struck at four o'clock. Screaming winds blew snow horizontally and plastered it against buildings, cars, trees, bison, and mountains. Inside Granddad's ranch house, the woodstove threw off its bone-warming heat. The Carlisles took up quiet activities. Grandma Sally sat close to the fire, doing a crossword puzzle. A smiling Granddad watched the bright dancing flames through the glass window of the stove. Blue Sky dozed on his knee. Charlie bent over a card table, thumbing through his notes.

"What're you doing?" Granddad finally asked.

"I'm looking for the perfect stone in my notes."

"That's a good start," Granddad commented.

"You're more mysterious than Blue Sky," Charlie said and turned back to reread an entry.

The telephone rang.

It was Singing Bird. Her voice was airy but serious. "Can I make a reservation tonight for three at the Night Care Center? We can't get to our woodpile, and the house is getting cold."

"Come on over," Charlie said. "Bring your schoolbooks. We may be here until spring."

And it was spring when the storm stopped—the raven's

spring. On January 4, Charlie opened the door and shov-eled his way upward from the porch to the top of the snow. He emerged in bright sunlight.

"Knock, knock." The call was given slowly and sensi-tively, then repeated three times. It was the love call of the raven. "Spring is here," the serenader had said.

Charlie squinted across the unspringlike landscape to lo-cate the raven. Although the sun on the snow was blinding, he picked out two ravens. They were sitting side by side on a limb of the big spruce near the pump house. They touched beaks, quorked at the sight of Charlie, and flew away. Charlie watched them climb high above the sagebrush flats, fold their wings simultaneously, and jet earthward. Near the ground they turned on their backs and sped upside down to Bison Butte. Charlie returned to his shoveling. "Spring," he said. "Some joke."

The snow was higher than the porch, and he had to shovel steps up from the porch to the top of the snowfall. Then he tramped a path to the snow-buried cars.

Jerry arrived. He was in the snowblower. His snowplow could not handle the deep drifts that the blizzard had piled up, so he had switched to the huge highway machine. Spraying geysers of crystals as he drove, he connected the Carlisles and the Kentons to the highways and towns again. Soon after they were freed, the Kentons departed for South Dakota.

Charlie fed Blue Sky, put him on Granddad's knee, and went to the sewing room to pack his books and clothes.

Grandma Sally was out of supplies and going to town. He would go with her. He had already missed two days of school. Even in blizzards, the Jackson schools opened, but he had not been able to get there.

With his pack stuffed full, he tiptoed past the living room, where Granddad and Blue Sky were dozing in front of the woodstove. He reached for the front doorknob. Feathers rustled. There was a whoosh of wings, and Blue Sky was on his shoulder.

"Okay, okay. You can come out." He touched the raven's glistening beak. "I don't know where you go when I'm gone, but someday I'll find out. And that will be the perfect round stone—and I will have earned my drum."

He opened the door and Blue Sky winged out over the white snow into the sun glare.

"There you go," said Charlie. "But where?"

Grandma was helping Granddad into his parka. She was not going to leave him alone. Charlie ran to the truck, cleaned off the snow, then went back and helped with Granddad.

"Can I take a quick look for Pinecone?" he asked Grandma when they had Granddad settled in the backseat. "I miss her."

"Well, hurry," she said. "I see a wind blowing snow across the flats. We'll get stuck in a drift if we don't leave now."

"Never mind," Charlie said and jumped in the truck. He knew perfectly well he would not see Pinecone. She too had gone where ravens go in winter.

They were almost to Sagebrush Flats Road when a bull moose leaped over a snow pile into their path. He completely filled the one-lane corridor between the banks of snow, so they had to stop the truck.

"Move!" Charlie called, and stepped out to chase the moose away. The huge animal reared and raised his enormous front feet with their cleaver-sharp hooves. He was ready to strike. Charlie got back in the truck and slammed the door shut. The moose struck, missed, then charged.

Grandma Sally backed up the truck.

The moose charged again. Grandma Sally backed up again. Then the moose lowered his head to contemplate the massive blue object before him. The great bell of fur that hung from his throat swung from side to side. His wide nostrils flared. He reared again, Grandma Sally backed the truck up to the gate, and he struck the air.

The moose calmed down and chewed an aspen twig. Grandma Sally waited for him to leave. Fifteen minutes passed. Charlie saw a raven alight on a telephone pole and tried to see if it wore bands. It was too far away to tell without binoculars. He sat back.

The wind blew snow high and higher and the moose turned to leave. Charlie opened the door to get out and help Granddad to the house. The moose scraped the snow with his front hooves, lowered his head, and ran straight at the open door. Grandma Sally backed up. The raven appeared and followed the moose.

Despite all that was going on, Charlie had time to be surprised to see a raven following a moose. He now knew ravens followed animals that could lead them to meat, but he couldn't imagine that a raven would want to eat the herbs and twigs that moose eat. He turned to Granddad. He was peering at the raven too.

"Things are really tough," Granddad said, "when a raven has to follow a moose—or—we have a raven who doesn't know a moose from a wolf."

"Pinecone?" suggested Charlie. "She might not know. She was partly raised by us. Has she ever come back since she left us?"

"Not to my knowledge," said Granddad. "I'm afraid she's met the fate of most of the young wild things."

"Oh, Will," said Grandma Sally. "Why do you have to say that?"

The moose stopped eating and faced the truck. He was determined to win this battle. The blue truck was mighty, but he, bull moose, was mightier.

"I guess we don't need supplies today," Grandma Sally said. "We'll open a can of soup."

"And I guess I don't need school today." Charlie cheered.

Grandma Sally backed the blue truck to the foot trail, earning enough distance and time to get Granddad out of the truck and into the house. The moose watched them, then turned and waded through snow up to his belly and ate Granddad's aspen twigs.

Inside the ranch house Grandma Sally called, "Anyone for canned soup?" and went to the cellar for the emergency rations without waiting for an answer.

Charlie and Granddad watched the moose through the kitchen window. They exclaimed over his magnificent antlers, which were four feet wide and three feet deep. They chuckled when his prehensile lip shot out like fingers and neatly picked the tender twigs.

"The old boy knew where he was going," Granddad said. "There goes the neighborhood."

"quork." Blue Sky was back. Charlie ran outside.

"And where did you come from?" he asked. "I saw you heading for the highway and the park or wherever you go when I'm gone. Or hey—that raven who was following the moose was not following the moose, he was following me—and it was you, Blue Sky, you!"

Blue Sky floated down to Charlie, rustling his feathers as he approached and rode inside on his shoulder.

"Granddad," Charlie called. "I think I know where Blue Sky goes when I'm not here."

"Where?"

"I'll have to run another experiment before I know for sure," he said. "It may take a little time."

Granddad's eyebrows went up, and his eyes twinkled.

CHAPTER SIXTEEN

The Perfect Round Stone

During the night new snow fell, and Grandma Sally put off her trip to Jackson again. When Jerry arrived in his snowplow Charlie asked to go back to town with him. The errant course of the snowplow from cabin to cabin, little town to ranch, was just the zigzag trek his new experiment required.

Blue Sky had come in for breakfast, and when Charlie let him out, he flew to the big cottonwood tree. There he preened his feathers, as if this were any weekend day. He was content. He did not fly west to the river bottomlands or to the nearby sagebrush flats to hunt. But when Charlie climbed into the cab of Jerry's snowplow, Blue Sky took off. He flapped hard over the yard, over the trees, and glided west toward Morton.

At Sagebrush Flats Road, Jerry turned east and headed for the little town. Good, thought Charlie, who was lying on the broad space behind the front seats, peering through the rear window for Blue Sky.

On either side of the road, the big mammals were declaring "winter" although the ravens were calling "spring." A herd of bison was huddled in a spot blown free of snow, the mule deer were eating aspen twigs instead of grass.

When Jerry turned into a horse rancher's property to plow his lane, Charlie jumped from the cab. A raven was circling low above the road.

Ha, he said to himself, I'm right, and focused his binoculars on the bird's legs. There were no bands. It was not Blue Sky.

"Aw, nuts," he said. "I don't know anything about ravens. I'm giving the drum back to Flying Cloud."

Discouraged, Charlie sat on the top rung of fence rail, which was still above the snow, and wondered what he should do now. A great horned owl called. Another answered.

"That means spring's here in the owl and raven world," he mused, "and they'll be nesting soon. They'll all be quiet and I'll never learn where Blue Sky goes."

Jerry came back to the road, stopped the snowplow, and picked up Charlie. He scrambled back up on the ledge behind the front seats. There he took up his scientific vigil, looking for Blue Sky. The snowplow rumbled down the road on the south side of Bison Butte. Charlie looked for mountain sheep posed against the skyline and wolf tracks coming down from the snowy crags. There were none, only snow and sky.

"Mighty lonely out here," he said.

"Except for that bird above the cab," Jerry replied.

"What bird?"

"It's black— a raven or a crow. I catch sight of it now and then in the rearview mirror. Is it your pet?"

"Wow! Maybe. Could you drive on for a short distance, then stop suddenly?" asked Charlie. "Maybe the bird will keep going when you stop." He slid into the passenger seat and stared out the front window.

When the snowplow halted, a raven flew on, as Charlie suspected it might. It circled and came back. Charlie saw the red band flash.

"Scalawag!" he shouted. "So that's how you travel to and from town without being seen!"

"What are you talking about?" Jerry asked.

"I'm talking about my raven pal, Blue Sky."

Jerry laughed. "You Carlisles are quite a clan. You are all really into nature. I know your uncle—the one who studies the cutthroat trout. You can't keep him out of a stream. And I saw your granddad nearly walk off a curb looking at some bird."

"Yeah," said Charlie.

"Want me to follow that raven?" Jerry asked.

"He follows us. You can go on to town. I know what I wanted to know. My raven stays out of sight above the truck or snowplow or whatever I'm in when I travel to town and back. That's why I've never seen him and that's why he appears out of nowhere at Granddad's ranch house. He's right there when I get there.

Now to find out where he gets food in town, Charlie wrote in his notebook.

When they reached the middle school Charlie got off the snowplow, and Blue Sky flew into a dense stand of spruce trees.

Charlie called hello to him, ran up the school steps, and dropped by the principal's office to tell him why he was three days late. The principal told him he wasn't the only one and waved him off to class.

As Charlie was listening to one of his classmates read a Gary Snyder poem, he noticed a large flock of ravens descending on the Dumpster behind the school cafeteria. "School leftovers," he said to himself. "So I do lead him to food."

When school was out, Charlie checked out the Dumpster. The ravens were gone—all but one. A single handsome individual sat on the school warm-ventilator pipe, his head lifted high, his horns up. Charlie thought he must be Blue Sky, but his pantaloons covered his leg bands. Charlie decided to walk home to see if this fellow followed him.

All along the way he stopped, looked up, walked, stopped, but he saw not one raven in the twenty minutes it took to get to his home at the foot of Snow King Mountain.

"But I know you're there, Blue Sky," he said and sat down on his porch to wait for him to show himself.

The next-door neighbor, Mrs. Crawford, stepped out on her patio and called to her cat, a wild thing that came and went around the neighborhood making a living where it could. She put down a large bowl of cat food and went back inside.

Charlie thought Mrs. Crawford might have scared away Blue Sky, and he set off to make a circuit of the neighborhood, searching trees and house tops for him. A few house sparrows were sheltered under eaves, but he saw no ravens.

After dinner he went to the room he shared with Andy and took out his homework. Presently some intuitive sense got him up from his chair and to the window. He picked up his binoculars and looked down on the patio. A raven was finishing off the cat food. He wore a red band on his leg.

Charlie ran downstairs and dialed the phone. Grandma Sally answered, then put Granddad on.

"Granddad," Charlie said, trying to be calm and professional. "I know where Blue Sky goes during the week."

"Tell me."

"To school and then to my house. He follows me." He paused. "And so, Granddad, I know what I am to Blue Sky."

"Tell me."

"His wolf."

Granddad was quiet for a long pause.

"That's a wonderful thing to be."

"I know I shouldn't say this," Charlie went on, "but ravens *are* uncanny. Every now and then they let a person see their magic. I am one of those persons."

"Hang on to that," Granddad said. "You're close to the perfect round stone."

"Aw, come on, what are you trying to tell me?"

"You'll see."

"Well, I see this. I am Blue Sky's wolf," Charlie said. "That's my perfect round stone."

"Keep looking," said Granddad. "Tell me, what do you lead him to?"

"The dumpsters at my school and Mrs. Crawford's cat food at home." He could hear Granddad chuckle. "Maybe that's why ravens like people," he said. "We've been leading them to food since we clobbered the first mammoth.

"By the way," said Granddad, "was Pinecone among that team of ravens?"

"I didn't see her." Then Charlie added quickly. "Have we finished the study? Can I write it up?"

"We still don't know where the young ravens go that don't follow you. Keep looking. And by the way, when you come out tomorrow, bring a half pound of twopenny nails, and wood glue. It's fix-it time."

"Does that mean you're better?"

"I'll feel a whole lot better when I fix Grandma's windowsill that the porcupine chewed and stop her grumbling."

During the winter months and right up to April, Blue Sky followed his boy-wolf by flying back and forth from town to ranch.

At the end of the first week of April, when the sage grouse were strutting to impress the hens with their eligibility as mates and the ground squirrels were up and about, Blue Sky changed his routine again. On April 9, he did not come to Granddad for greetings and breakfast, even when Charlie was there. Instead he sat on the roof ridge. He lifted his head feathers into a bonnet. He puffed out his throat and pantaloons feathers. He held his head high. On April 10, another raven flew into the cottonwood tree and perched within sight of him. Blue Sky did a graceful back-flip and roll, and flew to her side. They stepped close to each other. Blue Sky trilled, and his friend knocked. This went on for a long time. Charlie watched and wondered. Were they mates? Blue Sky was too young. It would be another year or so before he was old enough to breed. Could the female be Pinecone? He took a good look through Granddad's spotting scope—no bands. Since the new bird was not Pinecone, Blue Sky and this perky raven must be school sweethearts? He thought that sounded Good—so he wrote it in his journal.

Blue Sky "quorked" and "grrrrred" and made noises like people talk. "I hear you, Blue Sky. I know what you are saying. You're telling me good-bye."

"Write it down." And the two ravens flew away.

Charlie ran to Granddad.

"He talked to me. Blue Sky talked to me," he said. "He said good-bye. I know he did. He's gone."

"He might also have said he'd be back. Young ravens are recruiters. When one finds a carcass the resident adults attack it so ferociously it can't eat. So what does the youngster do? It goes out and recruits dozens of its peers and brings them back. The adults can't fend off an army, so they give up and let the juveniles eat."

"Good. That means Blue Sky might come back."

"That's what I'm hoping." Granddad looked somewhat smug. "I have another experiment going," he said. "I asked the park naturalist if he would leave roadkill in the sagebrush in front of my house," he said and grinned. "There's an elk there now. It's working like a charm. Come look."

Charlie peered through the spotting scope Granddad had set up. Two ravens were sitting on the carcass.

"Cool," said Charlie. "Who are the two birds?"

"Must be adults. I haven't seen young raven activity yet," Granddad said. "Those two drive away any ravens that approach the carcass. They're bundles of fury."

"They must be the Bison Butte pair," said Charlie. "The carcass is on their territory."

"I would say so for that very reason."

Unbeknownst to Charlie and Granddad, Blue Sky's mother had laid her first egg of the new season in the same nest in the same pine on Bison Butte. Only an army could force her and her mate to share the food on their territory now.

And that's just what happened. While Granddad and Charlie were talking, twenty or so young ravens came from the east, sailed over the house, and alighted on the sagebrush bushes around the elk carcass. Charlie looked through the scope. They were led by Blue Sky.

The Bison Butte adults did not defend their food. They took one look at the mob of juveniles—and let them approach the carcass. It was an iffy permission. The juveniles hopped toward the food and jumped back when the adults looked at them. They sidled up to the carcass, then nervously flew away. Finally the adults were overwhelmed by their numbers. They stopped lifting their horns and displaying their throat shackles to scare them off. And all settled down to eat. Granddad took out his notebook. "A lesson for mankind," he wrote. "Ravens battle—but do not kill their own kind."

While Charlie was staring at the raven show, he heard the rhythmical beat of horse hoofs and remembered that Mr. Spinder had telephoned he'd be returning to his ranch in April.

Charlie waited to hear the "KEK,KEK,KEK" alarm of the ravens when they saw their enemy. They did not call. The hoofbeats stopped in Granddad's yard. The ravens kept eating. Then a few young birds, having had their fill, flew into Granddad's trees. One sat low in a pine. It stared curiously at Mr. Spinder's horse. Charlie heard a knock and opened the door.

"Hi, ho, Charlie!" Al Spinder stood there. Still no alarm cry from the ravens.

Something had changed.

"I've got news that will make you and your granddad feel good." He stepped across the threshold. "Ravens are great." Charlie was completely taken aback. He did not expect to hear that. Then he remembered what Singing Bird had said on the night of the Teepee Festival: "Blue Sky is curing Granddad. Flying Cloud has cured Mr. and Mrs. Spinder."

Mr. Spinder had changed, not the ravens. He was now "friend," not "enemy." Charlie and Grandma Sally welcomed him, but he hurried past them and went straight to Granddad. He still wasn't very gracious.

"Will," he said, "you think you have stories to tell. Well—so do I." He pulled up a chair and loosened his bolo tie. Charlie and Grandma Sally stepped far enough into the living room to hear.

"After I left the Teepee Festival," Mr. Spinder began, " I felt eerie. I felt as if something had been washed out of me. My fear of ravens seemed to have gone."

Charlie's eyes widened. Mr. Spinder went on.

"I left Sagebrush Flats and joined my brother in the house on our tree farm that I told you about. He was all upset. Our investment was in peril. The trees were infested with an outbreak of army cutworms. They could kill the forest in a season. We had an expert come. He advised us to cut and burn. We had other experts advise us to spray. We didn't know what to do."

Granddad was nodding, as if expecting to hear this. Mr. Spinder went on.

"While we were debating, three ravens came to the woods. They looked around, made funny trilling noises, and went away. My brother went for his gun. I called your son, Chris, and asked him what to do. 'Nothing,' he said.

"Then the very next day hundreds maybe thousands of ravens came to our trees. The forest was black with them.

My fear of ravens returned wholesale—and I agreed with my brother to shoot every one and plead economic hardship. Then I saw what they were eating. Cutworms! Cutworms by the millions and probably billions! We waited and watched. They came back day after day until it seemed every cutworm in that forest was gone. You guys are right. They're nice birds. And I'm not afraid of them anymore."

"Do you know why you were afraid of them?" Granddad asked.

"Yeah, I do," Al Spinder said. "When I was little, I visited some relative in Maine. There were ravens there. They threw pinecones at me. My uncle told me they were evil and would pick out my eyes. I was terrified.

"I still think they're supernatural, rounding up hundreds of their kind and coming to my forest to clean out the cutworms like they did. But I don't think they're evil anymore. And that's the scientific fact I wanted to tell you." He rose to leave.

"Thank you," said Granddad and glanced at Charlie. "A big, big score in the Good column," Charlie said.

Charlie walked Mr. Spinder to his horse. The raven recruits were resting on the roof. Not one alarm was sounded.

"What I want to know," Charlie said when he was back with Granddad, "is how the ravens know Mr. Spinder has changed."

"Because," said Granddad, "the ravens are the perfect round stone. You'll never understand them. You'll never know all there is to know about them. But like the search for the perfect round stone, you'll always keep looking."

"What don't we understand about them—what makes ravens the perfect round stone?" Charlie asked.

Granddad ran his fingers through his thin hair, then down over his chin.

"Do we know whether Blue Sky knew my pills were bad or were they just pretty? Do we know why Blue Sky learned to speak English? Do we know why he tosses all the screws out of a can or pokes holes in rafts? Hungry or vindictive? We don't, and we never will know because the answer is in his raven mind."

"Are you saying I'll never find the perfect round stone because I am not a raven?"

"Yes, I am."

"Well," said Charlie. "I have an answer to my project and it is this. Ravens are neither Good nor Bad."

"Now," Granddad said, his eyes and cheeks puckered by his big smile, "you are ready to do research."

Charlie nodded. He now understood that scientific research was asking questions of nature and gathering information endlessly until you find the answer. It had nothing to do with Good or Bad.

"You've finished your study," Granddad said. "But I'll never see mine to its conclusion."

"You mean where young ravens go when they leave home?" Charlie asked. Granddad nodded.

"But we know where Blue Sky goes," Charlie said. "Isn't that enough?"

"What he does isn't wild behavior. Living with us has changed him."

"And he's changed us," Charlie said, scratching his head as he pondered. "Hey, I did do a study of the effect of the environment on people."

"I'm listening," said Granddad. "Tell me one effect."

"That I know enough about ravens to try to finish your study."

Granddad turned and looked out the window.

"To do that," he said, "you need radios and expensive equipment, even airplanes." He turned back to Charlie. "Unless," he said slowly, "you find Pinecone—or her bands turn up in a coyote dropping or a great horned owl casting. And that's one chance in a billion."

"I'll take it," said Charlie. "I'm going to keep looking for the perfect round stone."

CHAPTER SEVENTEEN

The Nest

The longer hours of daylight brought the wildflowers up through the ground and reconnected them with the stars and all the living things in between.

The aspen leaves unfolded, the antelope returned to the sagebrush flats. The elk followed the melting snow back to the alpine meadows. In the mountains the grizzly bears came down from their dens to fish and dig for yampa roots in the high meadows. The Bison Butte ravens fed their nestlings.

Like the migrant birds and the beasts, the Kentons returned to their summer home, and the teepee graced the landscape once more.

When the hummingbirds came back to nest, Granddad was moved to Chris's house in town to be closer to the doctor. Blue Sky did not come to the cabin that morning. Charlie told himself that the raven knew Granddad was ill and was looking for him.

May 16, he wrote. *I'm as spooky as Mr. Spinder. How can a bird know a man is sick?*

The summer passed. The days grew shorter and shorter. The least weasel that lived under Granddad's woodshed began to turn white, and the aspen leaves shone brilliant yellow, then fell to the ground.

Granddad was taken to the hospital. Chris drove, and Charlie and Grandma Sally rode in the backseat of the truck with him, although Charlie wished he could be somewhere else. He was frightened. Granddad had to go to the hospital. He had put the Raven Owners' drum in his pack. Charlie hoped it might help him find his "Warrior of Courage." Singing Bird had said there were many kinds of warriors—Warriors of Love, Warriors of Happiness, Warriors of Prosperity—and so he wanted to believe the Raven Owners' drum held his "Warrior of Courage." He needed to think that.

A few days after Granddad had been taken to the hospital, Singing Bird visited him with Charlie and Grandma. She wore her white deerskin dress, the one she wore only at teepee ceremonies. Charlie was about to tell her how beautiful she looked when he noticed she wore only one earring. He smiled. Singing Bird had given the other one to Blue Sky. She had never wanted it back.

"I have a story to tell," she said.

Granddad took her hand, pulled her to him, and kissed her cheek.

"Tell it," he said. "You tell important stories."

"You will hate it and you will love it." Without looking at Charlie she sat down beside Granddad. Charlie felt a wind as if from a nether world blowing down his spine. His hands grew cold. He reached for his drum.

"A long time ago a raven befriended a man. This friendship was not to the liking of the Raven Society, but Raven didn't care. He knew that raven and man could help each other. Man adopted him into his family and put a red band and an aluminum band on Raven's leg. That made him different from all other ravens. He liked that because he had a big ego. He soon became boss of his human family.

"Raven found man's food excellent and the company exciting. What really impressed Raven was that Man had all kinds of ways of getting food, with traps and can openers, fishing rods and bags of chow. The food was good and so abundant that Raven brought his friends to feast with Man. He even learned to talk like Man.

"But this was all one-sided. Raven could do nothing for Man. According to the ethics of the Ravens, if you are led to food by Man or Beast, you lead Man or Beast to food.

"But this Man didn't need Raven to lead him to food.

"Man had a grandson, and Raven and Grandson worked together in the raven way. Grandson led Raven to food. Raven led Grandson to food, although his tastes were strange. He never ate the mice and dung beetles Raven found for him.

"But Raven was a raven, and he still wanted to return the favors to Man not Grandson. Over and over he had heard Man say—where do young ravens go when they leave their parents? He knew this was important, but he didn't know how to show Man where they went because Man couldn't fly. Even if he could fly, he wouldn't know an adult raven from a young one. Man's eyes were very poor.

"One autumn day when Man was old he was moved into town, Raven missed him so much that he flew off with the young ravens.

"He flew forty miles east to the National Forests. There all the animals were getting ready for winter. The bears had made dens, the porcupines were leaving the lowlands for the pine forest. Men were hunting elk for winter food.

"Raven was hungry. He saw Al Elk Hunter in the forest. He would follow him to food.

"Two shots rang out. An elk dropped. Al Elk Hunter gutted the animal then walked miles to find his friend to help him butcher and pack the food out of the forest.

"When Al Elk Hunter was gone, Raven dropped down on the food. The adult resident ravens sped down from the mountaintop, claimed the carcass, and drove Raven away. He flew south, trilling and knocking and calling to his young friends to gang up on the residents.

"By twos and ones, fours and sevens and tens the young ravens came from miles away and followed Raven. They descended on the carcass. Their vast numbers overwhelmed the adult ravens. They gave up the fight, and young and old feasted.

"Presently Raven flew to the dead treetop to watch for enemies. He saw Al Elk Hunter and his friend, Big Elk Hunter, returning. Raven warned his friends with loud, frantic 'KEK's. The ravens flew away.

"A shot rang out. Raven fell to earth.

"Big Elk Hunter walked to the dead raven he had shot.

He saw bands on its legs and took them off. He gave the bands to Al Elk Hunter. When he returned home, he gave the bands to Storyteller, and Storyteller has brought them to you, dear Man of Legend."

In Singing Bird's palm lay a red and an aluminum band. She put them in Granddad's hand. He stared long, then closed his fingers over them.

"Blue Sky has completed my research," he said softly. His eyes grew misty. Charlie clutched his drum to stop the pain in his heart. As he ran his hand across it, he felt the presence of his Warrior of Courage and took him in. When he at last could look at Granddad the old naturalist was smiling.

"That's an unbelievable story," he said. "And I wouldn't

believe it except that some uncanny magic radiates from ravens.

"And Charlie, you can write that down."

"I will."

With the Warrior of Courage inside him and the Raven Owners' drum on his lap, Charlie handed Granddad a piece of paper.

"I have finished my study too," he said. "Here is my report. I don't think the National Science Foundation will like it, but you might." Granddad took the paper in his thin hands, then handed it to Grandma Sally.

"Please read it to me, Sal," he said.

"It's three columns of data," she said. "Good, Bad, and Mysterious."

RAVEN CHECKLIST

GOOD	*BAD*	*MYSTERIOUS*
Tool users	Throws things	Morphed from pine needles into a raven
Throws things	Throws things	Throws things
Granddad snaps to attention at sound of baby raven	Steals and hides earring	Six ravens on a roof
		Knows enemy is Mr. Spinder
Knows enemy is Mr. Spinder		Performs ballet
Yells at Mr. Spinder	Destroys letters	Appears from nowhere

GOOD	BAD	MYSTERIOUS
Gets his own way	Gets his own way	Gets his own way
Bonds with Charlie	Pokes holes in raft	Pokes holes in raft
Knows death	Knows death	Knows death
Shares food	Shreds recipe	Speaks English
Gives gifts	Dumps screws	Does not come to breakfast
Likes pretty things	Likes pretty things	Likes pretty things
Likes wolf	Whacks Nancy's shoe	Lets Charlie know he wants routine
Recognizes individual people	Messes up shingle	
		Friends with wolf
	Pulls up lettuce	
Cleans up carcasses	Steals	Has new relationship with Charlie
School sweethearts		Hunts on Mr. Smiley's roof
Parents chase off young	Parents chase off young	Parents chase off young
Eats cutworms		
		Appears and disappears
		Uncanny knowledge

Grandma Sally folded the paper and returned it to Charlie.

"That's an amazing list," she said with pride in her voice. "But where's the mountain lion? You didn't even mention the drama of the mountain lion. Why isn't that in the Good column?"

Granddad lifted his heavy eyelids and looked at Charlie, waiting expectantly for his answer.

Charlie held his drum closer to his chest, knowing that what he was going to say could cost him his beloved Raven Owners' drum.

"Because," he said slowly, looking straight at Granddad, "I'll never find the answer to that—it's the perfect round stone."

On the way home from the hospital, Charlie hurt too much to speak. Blue Sky was dead. He felt as if his heart had been ripped from his body, and he did not know how to stop the pain. His Warrior of Courage was fiction. He did not exist. Then Grandma Sally drove around a bend, and there in the warm unfrozen stream that flowed through town, glided the two beautiful white trumpeter swans. Charlie sat up and stared at them.

For some reason or other, he said to himself, they didn't fly south for the winter. Have they stayed to take Blue Sky's place? Everything lately has been mysterious, so I'm going to say so. It makes me feel better.

Charlie watched the beautiful birds until the truck rounded a bend and they were out of sight.

———

In late October, Granddad was laid to rest among the wild-flowers on Sagebrush Flats. Three bald eagles flew into his big cottonwood tree and sat upright and silent. A rough-legged hawk, on his way south, rested on the chimney of his house. Granddad's mountain bluebird, who had been reluc-tant to migrate and leave the abundant autumn crickets, posed on its favorite aspen twig. When the gathering of peo-ple stopped speaking and singing and the ceremony was over, the bird read the angle of the sun's rays and flew south.

Not far from Granddad's grave, a dandelion bloomed in the light cover of snow.

The winter was long and severe. Charlie came out week-ends to help Grandma Sally with the chores. The Kentons stayed on Sagebrush Flats for the winter, and Grandma Sally helped Flying Cloud edit his book. As she worked, she wrote down the wisdoms of the Teton Sioux and posted them over the sink beside Charlie's Raven Checklist. They helped her through the lonely days.

One weekend while shoveling snow, Charlie suggested to Grandma Sally that they put raven food out on the roof again.

"The ravens might cheer us up," he said.

"Not yet," she answered. "I'm not ready for ravens yet. Are you?"

"No," he said softly. "I'm not." His hand had found the

red and the aluminum bands in his pocket, and he was fighting back tears.

On December 21, Flying Cloud celebrated the winter solstice, and life on earth began to change. As far away as South America, the birds felt the length of the day change. They began moving slowly northward. Although the ground was still covered with snow, Charlie stepped out of the ranch house one morning to see Granddad's mountain bluebird wing across the yard and return to his favorite twig. When he threw back his head and sang, Charlie knew his sadness would end.

In late February a blizzard slammed snow against the sagebrush, trees, and ranch house, and Charlie and Grandma Sally couldn't see out the windows. When the storm stopped they snowshoed around the house, clearing the windows and letting in sunlight.

They had worked their way back to the porch when Charlie touched Grandma's arm and pointed. Two ravens were diving headfirst toward the earth, one close behind the other. They looped, shot skyward, rolled upside down, and dove again. They touched wings.

"Raven spring," he said.

"Oh, Charlie, now it's time to put out raven food." Grandma Sally smiled and shook snow from her hair. "I'm ready."

Up over the ranch house and down into the yard came a glistening black raven. She carried a stick in her beak. Close behind came her mate. They flew into Granddad's tall spruce tree.

"Charlie," whispered Grandma. "Could it be that we will be honored with nesting ravens?"

"I doubt it," he said. "They never nest this close to people—but ravens radiate magic."

Charlie ran into the house and brought back Granddad's spotting scope. He focused it on the raven. She was arranging the stick in her nest.

"Grandma," he whispered. "Pinecone's back!"

Raven Glossary

boing	call to wolf
ca,ca,ca,ca,ca	anger
feather rustle	"Don't bother me." / "You're disturbing me."
gro, gro, gro	"Feed baby raven."
grrrrr	comfort call
KEK,KEK,KEK,KEK,KEK	alarm cry
kmmmm grrr/kmmmm gurgle	"I love you."
knock, knock, knock	power call / "Look at me."
knock trill	adult food call
quork! quork! quork! (3 times fast)	call in defense of home territory
QUORK! QUORK! QUORK!	more intense call: "Get out of here! My territory!"
quork, quork, quork, trilllll	recruiting call: "Food here! Come eat!"
single quork	"Mine."
undulating quorks (several quorks in succession)	"I'm here. Take notice."
REK,REK,REK,REK,REK	intense exclamation

Literature Circle Questions

Use the questions and activities that follow to get more out of the experience of reading *Charlie's Raven* by Jean Craighead George.

1. What is wrong with Charlie's grandfather? Why does Charlie think a raven will help?

2. Where does Charlie find the raven? What happens when he takes it from the nest?

3. What does Charlie feed Blue Sky when he first brings him home?

4. What sorts of calls does Blue Sky make to Charlie and his grandfather? What sorts does he make to the Spinders? Why are they different?

5. Summarize what happens when Grandma faces the mountain lion. How do you interpret Blue Sky's behavior? Do you think it was good or bad?

6. Give some examples of Granddad feeling better. Why do you think this is?

7. Mr. Spinder's attitude toward ravens changes throughout the book. What is his attitude at first? What makes him change his mind?

8. The different raven calls mean many different things. Are there ways in which people communicate with more than words? Do any of the characters do this?

9. The different characters in the book all have their own reasons for interpreting the behavior of ravens. Explain these differences and discuss where their ideas originate.

10. What is the "perfect round stone"?

11. What are some examples of Blue Sky's behavior that can be considered both good and bad? Can you think of anything else that can be both good and bad? Explain your reasons.

12. Suppose Charlie spent his summers with the Spinders instead of with his grandparents. What might his "perfect round stone" be in that case?

13. On pages 64–65, the parent ravens are observed dropping off and picking up Pinecone as if the cabin is a day care center. Do you think it is accurate to say that the ravens are really thinking about it in this way? Explain.

14. Reread Singing Bird's story, on pages 69–70, about how the raven's cure works. Is this a story about magic, or is it a story about science? Can it be both? Explain.

15. When Charlie worries about how Blue Sky will take care of himself, Granddad says, "He'll take care of himself, or he won't. That's how all life is." Do you think this opinion is harsh? What do you think makes Granddad come to this conclusion?

Note: These questions are keyed to Bloom's Taxonomy as follows: Knowledge: 1–3; Comprehension: 4–6; Application: 7–8; Analysis: 9–10; Synthesis: 11–12; Evaluation: 13–15

Activities

1. Create your own animal vocabulary. The glossary at the back of the book lists several raven calls and their corresponding meanings. Choose an animal (or make up one of your own) and invent a list of sounds to communicate different meanings. Think about what you will need to say to others in order to be happy, healthy, and comfortable.

2. Take scientific notes, as Charlie does in the book. You can study birds, a favorite pet, or members of your own family. Make a log sheet or use a small notebook. Put down the date, time, and location of your observation.
   Try to be objective. Try not to assume a purpose for the behavior at this time. When your observations are complete, go back and review your notes and "let the data speak." Look for patterns and trends. What do you notice?

3. On pages 36–37, Charlie learns about the Raven Owners, a tribe whose totem animal was the raven. Form your own tribe with its own totem animal or thing. What is it about your totem that displays the special qualities of your tribe? How would your totem help or protect you?

Other books by this author include:

My Side of the Mountain, *Frightful's Mountain*, and *Julie of the Wolves* (all published by Dutton Children's Books, a division of Penguin Young Readers Group).

Author Web site: www.jeancraigheadgeorge.com